COLD SPRING

COLD SPRING

Patrick McGinley

NEW ISLAND

COLD SPRING
First published 2013
by New Island
2 Brookside
Dundrum Road
Dublin 14

www.newisland.ie

PRINT ISBN: 978-1-84840-220-1
EPUB ISBN: 978-1-84840-222-5
MOBI ISBN: 978-1-84840-221-8

British Library Cataloguing Data. A CIP catalogue record for this
book is available from the British Library

Typeset by JVR Creative India
Cover design by Nina Lyons
Printed by Bell & Bain Ltd., Glasgow

New Island received financial assistance from
The Arts Council (An Comhairle Ealaíon), Dublin, Ireland

10 9 8 7 6 5 4 3 2 1

For my grandson Owen

Acknowledgement

I would like to thank my brother-in-law Francie O'Donnell for his help with the details of sheep farming and lambing.

1

No one lives in Leaca any more. What was once a lively townland has become a place of roofless houses and overgrown laneways, a hunting-ground for the resident crows and foxes. Now and again two or three lobster fishermen put in at the little slip and eat a frugal lunch undisturbed. Leaca has become a place of solitude, sought out occasionally by hillwalkers in search of peace, or bird-watchers contemplating the movements of gannets and cormorants. The terrible events of the spring of 1948 are forgotten.

In that year Leaca was already in a state of irreversible decline. The young people had fled to Dublin or emigrated to England, Scotland or America. Only eight men and three women remained; middle-aged or elderly. They had known one another since childhood, and had learnt to tolerate one another's quirks and eccentricities. For the most part they lived like their forefathers, supplementing fishing with sheep farming and vice versa. They did not lack for life's necessaries, but neither did they enjoy many of its luxuries. All they asked for was good health and a full belly, and most of the time they told themselves that they had little cause for complaint.

What they knew about the great world was what they had gleaned from the local newspaper, and that did not impress them. They rarely talked about the news in the headlines; their interest lay in the daily round of work and the life of the larger community in the lower glen. All of them were accomplished historians of one another's families, a skill that had been passed down from father to son and from mother to daughter for at least seven generations. The personal qualities they treasured were generosity, reliability, resourcefulness and physical prowess. Anyone who was self-seeking or born outside the tribe was treated with covert reserve.

Red Miller was one such man. He was a successful sheep farmer and he was easy to talk to, yet among his neighbours he had a reputation of being 'out for himself'. His father and grandfather were said to have been 'tight', and his great grandfather, an English coastguard called Habakkuk Miller, got a local girl in the family way and then skedaddled without marrying her. Since Red Miller was a direct descendant of Habakkuk, everyone believed that he had inherited the bad blood of his exotically named ancestor, and when he fell out with his nearest neighbour Paddy Canty over trespassing sheep, they all backed Canty. Paddy Canty was eighty-six, they said. He was the oldest man in Leaca and could not be expected to run after every sheep that strayed. To make matters worse, Red Miller's dog tore the throat out of one of Canty's ewes. People shook their heads and said it was only what they had expected. The name Habakkuk was muttered darkly, and when Red Miller's dog disappeared mysteriously one night, everyone agreed that a dog that worried sheep was no great loss to anyone.

The only other man who did not belong to the self-appointed circle of old cronies was the young Englishman, Nick Ambrose. He and his partner Sharon McElwee first came to Leaca over two years ago. Nick did not shave. He sported a heavy stubble, and wore his black curly hair long. When asked what he did for a living, he would say that he and Sharon were both idealists; that they were escaping from the city and people who know nothing about anything apart from handling other people's money. Here they would live simply and quietly, in tune with nature and the ancient wisdom of the earth. They bought an old stone-built byre from Red Miller, which they extended and re-roofed. They plastered and whitewashed the stonework and made a snug little two-room cottage with one door and three windows. There they lived together, except when Sharon went off to Dublin for a week to sell her paintings, leaving Nick to take care of their six-year-old daughter Emily.

Nick was not a good provider. He never grew enough potatoes and vegetables for their needs, and he omitted to cut an adequate supply of turf in spring, with the result that he was reduced to beachcombing for cast-in during the winter or picking up bits of timber and dead branches for firewood on his walks. Sometimes he would earn a few shillings help-ing his aging neighbours with sheep shearing, lambing or dipping, but what little income they could depend on came from the sale of Sharon's paintings. As she liked a drink, a sizable share of her earnings went on whiskey. Whenever he reminded her of this inconvenient fact, she would tell him that the money she earned was hers, and that if he fancied bacon for dinner he would have to bring it home himself.

To give Nick his due, he wasn't lacking in ambition. He longed to become a successful writer, and he liked to tell her about the places they would visit when his ship finally came in. He wrote poems and short stories, but as he rarely managed to sell them Sharon advised him to take up serious drinking instead. In his own defence he said that it was not unknown for great artists to live in penury. It was early days, he reminded her. At his age Vermeer was still unheard of. Like Vermeer, he himself was a slow worker. Vermeer had left less than forty paintings. Significantly, he died in debt and didn't become famous until two hundred years after his death.

'Two hundred years!' Sharon scoffed. 'Even two hundred days would try my patience.' Sharon would wait for no man. She knew her own mind and there was nothing he could do to change it.

Coming up to nine o'clock on a cold and foggy evening in March 1948 the men of the townland met in Paddy Canty's house. Everyone was there, apart from Red Miller and Nick Ambrose, neither of whom had passed the Man of Leaca test. Daniel Burke, the retired schoolmaster, was first to arrive. Then came Tom Barron, Muiris Mór O'Donnell, Marcus Quinn, Cormac Gildea, and finally, Neil Durkin. Paddy produced a bottle of Powers from the dresser and gave them all a glass. He said that he drank nothing but Powers because at his age it was the only whiskey he could taste. The rest, he said, was strictly for youngsters under seventy-five. Then he turned to Muiris and asked him to be *fear a' tí*, master of ceremonies, for the occasion.

Muiris was twelve years younger than Paddy. He was tall and sinewy and had lost none of his bulk. His craggy face was weather-beaten, and his bony nose and high forehead suggested a keenly scrutinising mind. He spoke slowly and clearly. He was seen by the others as one of nature's leaders, a thinking man who meant what he said and never uttered a foolish word or a word he had to retract.

'Paddy asked for this meeting,' he began. 'Like the rest of us, he notices things missing about the house. Turf gone from the shed. Potatoes gone from the barn. Turnips gone from pits. How many of you have noticed what I'm talking about?'

'We all notice things,' the schoolmaster replied. 'Small things, sometimes so small you can't be sure they've been taken.'

'Small things still add up,' Marcus Quinn said.

'It isn't the value; it's the nuisance of never being sure. Sometimes I think I'm only imagining things,' Paddy complained.

'You're not imagining it,' Muiris reminded him. 'The question is, who's doing it?'

'We all know who's doing it,' Cormac Gildea said. 'No one but a foreigner would live on a bog and think of stealing turf.'

'I wouldn't mind if he wasn't the strongest man in Leaca, apart maybe from Red Miller himself,' Neil Durkin smiled.

Neil was a weaver who worked indoors for the most part. He looked paler than the others, and was less robust.

'Well, we know the culprit,' Paddy said. 'So what are we going to do about it?' He took out his empty pipe and began sucking it with his finger in the bowl. He had given up tobacco for Lent but not the empty pipe.

'Do we really know the culprit?' the schoolmaster asked. 'We won't know for certain till we've caught him in the act.'

'There's such a thing as likelihood,' Muiris said. 'Who needs turf the most? Who needs potatoes, turnips, eggs? And which of us would put another man's chicken in his own pot? We're all sensible and honest. We've lived here all our lives. We never lost as much as an egg before Ambrose came. Is that not certainty enough for you?'

'If we're certain, we need to speak to him,' Tom Barron said. 'And if we speak to him, he'll only deny it. As Daniel said, we need to catch him in the act.'

'That's it. Catch him red-handed,' Cormac said. 'If we catch him, we'll come down on him like a ton of bricks.'

'Who's going to catch him?' Muiris looked round at his neighbours. 'A thief comes in the night. At our age none of us is going to sit up all night waiting.'

'We'll lay a trap for him,' Neil Durkin said. 'We'll put temptation in his way and see if he can resist it.'

'All this is wild talk,' the schoolmaster said. 'The whole thing could be someone having a joke or trying to get Ambrose into trouble.'

'Now, which of us would be mad enough to do a thing like that?' Muiris wanted to know.

'No one here,' Marcus Quinn said.

'Could it be Red Miller, then?' Paddy Canty wondered, as if taken by a sudden shaft of enlightenment. 'He'd do it, be the hokey, if he thought it would get us all at each other's throats.'

'The truth is we don't really know who's doing it, so how can we pass judgement?' the schoolmaster said.

'I don't agree.' Muiris raised his index finger. 'We all know in our hearts who's doing it but no one is willing to accuse him to his face. At least, not yet. We'll sleep on it and allow our thoughts and hearts to harden. We'll give him more rope. The boot hasn't really started to pinch. When one of you loses a year-old wether, you'll soon change your tune. We'll meet at my place on Monday evening. In the meantime keep an eye on your belongings and try to find out what you think.'

'In ancient Ireland poets lived on the people,' Daniel said. 'Maybe we should feel honoured to have two artists living among us. Who knows, they may put Leaca on the map one day.'

'Artists, my arse!' Muiris said. 'They're good for no one but themselves. Look at that painting on the wall there. It's supposed to be me. Now look at it and tell me if it's anything like the man you all know.'

Cormac and Marcus Quinn laughed. Neil Durkin slapped his thigh and joined in the merriment.

'You mean the man I think I know?' Daniel said seriously.

'What are you talking about?' Muiris demanded.

'Artists paint from the inside out. That's how Sharon thinks you'd look if your face reflected what goes on inside your head.'

'So I think like a gorilla, then! Is that what you mean?'

'Enough's enough,' Paddy Canty said, going around again with the whiskey bottle. 'I've never heard such nonsense in all my life.'

He put an armful of black turf on the fire and they settled down to a good grumble about the north wind and the cold weather. They wondered how long it would last and discussed the effect a prolonged spell of frost would have on the lambing. None of them was getting any younger. It was a bad time to fall out with Ambrose. His help would be needed with the lambing, not to mention the digging and sowing.

After a while the conversation petered out. A live coal rolled onto the hearth and Muiris reached for the tongs.

'You're keeping us all in suspense, Paddy.' Muiris dropped the coal in the centre of the fire.

'Suspense about what?' Paddy asked slyly.

'The young woman who came to see you today,' Cormac said. 'I wish a young woman would come to see me.'

'That's not the suspense I meant,' Muiris said emphatically.

'She was a fine specimen of a woman,' Cormac continued. 'I was in the field fornenst the house when I saw this white car coming up the brae. Someone for the schoolmaster, I thought, but the car didn't stop at Daniel's. Straight up the road it went, past Neil's and past Tom's till it landed outside Paddy's door.'

Muiris clenched his teeth, which was his way of expressing outright disapproval.

'I suppose you were expecting her?' Marcus enquired.

'Well, to tell you the truth, I wasn't,' Paddy said seriously.

'You must have got a shock, then.' Daniel suggested.

'I got a pleasant surprise.'

'She was a fine young lady,' Neil Durkin agreed. 'I got a glimpse of her legs as she got out of the car. That one knows a thing or two, I said.'

Muiris grunted and knocked out his pipe on the hearth. He blew through the mouthpiece with a whistling sound, before reaming the bowl with his penknife. Looking magisterially round the kitchen, he seemed to indicate that the conversation was several notches beneath his contempt.

'She must be very important to go about in a white car,' Cormac said.

'Well, to be honest, I never noticed the car,' Paddy smiled.

Muiris groaned, unable to conceal his impatience any longer. He cut a wedge of plug tobacco into his wide palm, then minced and rubbed it with due ceremony. Finally, he filled his pipe with exaggerated care so that no shred of tobacco was lost.

'We all know you, Paddy,' Neil Durkin joked. 'It wasn't the car that was on your mind.'

'You're right there,' Paddy agreed. 'At my age a man needs to show a sail in every wind that blows.'

Muiris took a live coal from the fire with the tongs and held it over the bowl. Then he drew on his pipe with a smacking noise until the tobacco glowed and smoke began to pour from his nostrils.

'Did she say who she was?' Daniel asked.

'Well, would you believe it, I never thought of asking her.'

'She was with you for over an hour. You had a long confab, I'll bet,' Marcus probed.

'An hour, did you say? It only felt like five minutes.'

Muiris removed the pipe from between his lips and inhaled a mouthful of smoke. He was accustomed to commanding the attention of his neighbours, yet the lighting of his pipe seemed to have gone entirely unnoticed.

'She must have been very good-looking.' Neil Durkin winked at Cormac.

'She was so good-looking that I lost the thread of what she was saying to me.'

'She'll be coming again, I suppose?' Cormac speculated.

'She said she'd like to, but you know what women are like.'

'You can't believe a word they say, and some men aren't much better.' Muiris slapped his thigh and got to his feet.

'What suspense did you mean, Muiris?' Paddy, like the rest of them, knew that Muiris wasn't slow to take offence.

'I heard you had words with Red Miller this morning. They say his bull broke through your fence to get at the wee red heifer. Can that be true now?'

'We had words, certainly. And not for the first time either. But to be honest, the comely young woman drove himself and his bull clean out of my mind.'

Muiris reached for his stick and turned up the collar of his jacket around his ears. 'Good night, Paddy,' he said. 'Next time she comes, send her over to me. I'll ask her why she didn't come like Niamh on a white horse.'

There was silence in the kitchen as they listened to his retreating footsteps in the yard.

'Muiris left a bit sudden,' Cormac said.

'He's a man of sudden decisions,' Daniel smiled.

'It could be his kidneys troubling him,' Tom Barron conjectured.

'You mean his bladder?' Daniel said.

'Or his big toe.' Paddy laughed. 'We all know Muiris. He doesn't like any talk about women. It's his great failing. He can only talk about men.'

The steam had gone out of the conversation. After a while, Cormac said it was nearly bedtime. One by one they took their leave, all except Tom Barron who lingered in the hope that Paddy might tell him about Red Miller. Paddy was in no mood to talk about bulls and heifers. All he could think of was the young woman.

'She'll be coming to see me again,' he boasted. 'I offered to make her a cup of tea but she said she'd make me one instead. So I gave her the tea box and the teapot and watched her bustling about the kitchen like any housewife. She made good strong tea, fair play to her. I put a drop of whiskey in mine but she said she'd have hers straight from the pot. No milk, no sugar. She laughed when I told her she was cheap to run.'

Tom got up and said goodnight. He couldn't help wondering if Paddy in his old age was going a bit soft in the head. On the way home he kept clenching his fists to keep his fingers from freezing. He smelt fog, breathed fog and tasted fog on his tongue. It was so thick that he could see only a few yards in front of him. Even the lights in the windows of the houses were barely visible. The fog stole in under his clothes and seeped through the pores of his skin into the very marrow of his bones. At least he wasn't going home to a cold bed. Nancy would put two hot water bottles between the sheets because they both suffered from cold feet at night. Nancy blamed it on poor circulation. He himself put it down to advancing years. He had never had cold feet as a young man.

After Tom had gone, Paddy raked the fire and went to bed. The sheets were like ice. He missed Mary, even though it was now four years since she died. They had been married forty-seven years with never a harsh word spoken. He lay on his back and pulled the bedclothes up under his chin, grateful for the fire of the whiskey in his belly. Before he fell asleep, he thought he saw the face of the young woman looking down at him from the darkness overhanging the bed.

He woke and raised his head from the pillow, wondering if he'd heard a sound. It could have been a stray gust of wind in the chimney, though it was calm as he went to bed. There it was again, a creaking sound this time, not one of those natural sounds from the shore he was so used to hearing in the night. For a moment the faraway cry of a curlew distracted him. It was a lonely cry that made him wish for the company of Tom Barron and the others. The fire of the whiskey in his stomach had died down. As he flung back the bedclothes, the cold of the small hours gripped him in the groin. It was pitch-dark in the room. No glimmer of light came from where the window should be. He cocked an ear again. This time the sound was unmistakable. It had come from the kitchen, as if someone had stumbled over the creepie stool. He got down on his hands and knees and reached in under the bed where he kept his toolbox. Careful not to make a sound, he searched desperately for a weapon of defence. Then the bedroom door creaked behind him and he knew he was no longer alone in the room.

2

*T*om Barron scooped out the last of the white from the eggshell. Putting another egg in the eggcup, he immediately topped it with his spoon. He had an aggressive way with an egg. While her father used to tap and tap rather gently, Tom would make a drive with the tip of the spoon. Nancy always gave him the brown eggs. She kept the white ones for herself, not because she preferred them, but in order to please him. He couldn't really say why he preferred brown eggs. His mother gave him the brown ones as a boy, probably because she herself preferred the white ones, and when he got married, Nancy soon learned to do the same.

'It's an odd vagary,' she once remarked. Then, thinking that he might take offence, she quickly said that it was harmless enough and that she didn't mind the white ones. Men had their ways. It was well known that Red Miller couldn't abide marmalade. The only jam he'd thank you for was blackcurrant. Once, when his wife came back from the shop with a pot of marmalade, he took the pot from her hand and let it drop to the floor. Tom, thank heavens, was a civilised man. He never uttered a wrong word in her hearing. When there were no brown eggs, he simply went without. Once she fried him two white ones instead, thinking he wouldn't notice. He looked at the plate and then at her.

'White or brown?' he asked.

'White, I'm afraid. I thought you wouldn't mind them fried.'

'Well, I do,' he said. 'Neither make nor break a custom.'
Then he smiled at her and slid the eggs onto her plate with
his knife.

This morning she watched him put a knob of butter in
the second egg to soften it. The second egg was always a little
harder than the first, and she knew that was not how he liked
it. She had offered to boil them separately, so that the second
egg would be ready only when he had eaten the first, but he
said that it was far too much trouble and that anyway it was
impossible to get two eggs to boil exactly the same. When
she suggested that he top both eggs together, he said that the
second one would get cold while he was eating the first. A
second egg was like a second cup of tea, never as good as the
one before. It was a fact of life, one of those little things we
could do nothing about. It was best to accept them, because
life was never meant to be perfect. That's what she liked about
Tom, his way of looking at things which was always the way
of reason and commonsense. She waited for him to say something about the meeting the previous evening. He finished
the second egg and buttered a slice of her homemade soda
bread. As she poured him another mug of tea, she knew there
was something fretting his mind.

'How did the meeting go?' She finally realised that he
wasn't going to mention it without a little prompt from her.

'A lot of talk about next to nothing.'

'It must have been about something.'

'That was the trouble. We couldn't be absolutely sure.
Some said it was about Red Miller, others that it was about
Nick Ambrose. The only thing we could agree on was that it
was about whoever is stealing turf and eggs and potatoes. It
was Paddy Canty's idea, having the meeting. He's getting old,
poor man. Every little thing gets on his nerves.'

'And what decision did you come to?'

'None. Muiris said we should all go away and think about
it. We're having another meeting on Monday.'

'Muiris loves meetings. He likes to hear himself talk.'

He said no more. She could tell he was holding back whatever was on his mind.

'Whoever is doing it is a nuisance,' she said. 'I keep losing eggs, and it's always the brown ones that go. Daniel's wife lost a chicken last week, and it wasn't the fox that took her. She was taken from the henhouse with the door hasped.'

They both looked up as the yard gate squealed on its hinges. A burly man came through with his head lowered like a butting ram. In his right hand he carried a blackthorn, which he slashed against his right boot at every second step.

'Red Miller,' she said. 'Will you look at the cut of him!'

'He was always an early riser.'

'What can he want at this hour of the morning?'

The porch door opened. A shadow fell across the kitchen floor as Red Miller paused on the threshold.

'Anyone up?' he called.

'One or two,' Tom replied.

'Bad news, I'm afraid. Paddy Canty passed away in the night. I called in to see him about the broken fence. He was sitting in his armchair in his drawers with his head like this on his chest. It must be ages since I stood inside his house. The place looked like it was hit by a hurricane.'

'What do you mean?' Tom got up and reached for his hat.

'Nothing where it should be. Everything strewn on the floor.'

'I left Paddy at bedtime last night. The kitchen was spick and span, and he was his usual hearty self.'

'It's no lie I'm telling. Come and see for yourself.'

'This is terrible news,' Nancy said. 'Paddy will be missed. He was as hardy as a snipe. I thought he'd live to see the hundred.'

'It shocked me,' Red Miller said. 'We all know we must die but we like to live as if it will never happen.'

'Dying was the last thing on Paddy's mind. His thoughts were on living last time I saw him.'

She watched from the window as they both crossed the yard. Red Miller was broad and thickset, shapeless in his bulky clothes. Tom was tall and well built, and he bore himself erect. Even now in his late sixties you'd know he was once a fine figure of a man.

The two men didn't say much on the way to Paddy Canty's. Though they'd never had occasion to cross each other, they weren't friends. Whenever they met, they talked only about things that mattered to neither of them. Tom wouldn't dream of asking Red Miller's opinion of a ram, for example, and Red Miller was equally distant with him. Now they confined their conversation to occasional remarks about work and the freezing weather.

'It's still like the dead of winter,' Red Miller said. 'It would freeze the drop at the end of your nose.'

Tom Barron gave this observation some thought because at first he was uncertain how to respond to it.

'If this cold spell lasts, everything will be very late this year,' he said with a little sigh.

As soon as he entered Paddy Canty's kitchen, he knew that something terrible had happened. Clothes and newspapers were strewn on the floor. Paddy was seated in his armchair in the corner with his head on his chest, his hair tousled and his cheeks grey. His hand was cold to the touch; the thought that he must have died shortly after he'd left him was both puzzling and disturbing. As he raised his chin on his palm, he noticed the dark-blue line on his neck.

'He didn't die a natural death, poor man.' Tom spoke quietly, as if to himself.

'You think he died a violent death?'

'I'm sure of it. Look at that mark on his neck.'

'He gave me the shock of my life,' Red Miller said. 'I never even noticed it.'

Tom tried to visualise the kitchen as it was the previous evening. An empty bottle of Paddy whiskey now stood on the form by the door. The fire on the hearth was covered in

ash, and little wisps of smoke rose from the turf sods that surrounded it. The bedroom door was open, and Paddy's trousers
with the braces attached were draped over the back of a chair
while his white cable-stitch sweater lay across the seat. He
looked into the bedroom where more chaos met his eye. The
bedclothes lay in a twisted heap on the floor and a club ham-
mer lay where the pillow should have been.

'Do you think it was a robber that did it?' Red Miller
asked.

'We'd better not disturb anything till the guards come,'
Tom said.

They closed the door behind them and walked back
down the lane in the direction of the schoolmaster's house.
The schoolmaster had a car, the only car in Leaca. He would
drive to the village and alert the police. Red Miller was gab-
bling excitedly. He kept going over the scene that confronted
him when he first entered Canty's kitchen, as if seeking to
find a reason why he had failed to spot the mark on his neck.
Tom listened, for the most part in silence. He felt perplexed
and rather shaken. Paddy was his oldest friend. They'd farmed
together and fished together, and on fair days, when the business of buying and selling was done, they ended up drinking
together. Paddy was a lovely old man. He couldn't believe
that anyone in his right mind would wish him harm.

After leaving the schoolmaster's, Red Miller said he'd
tell the other neighbours the sad news. Tom went home to
Nancy, who was ironing his Sunday shirt. When he told her
what he'd seen, she put down the iron and she raised both her
hands to her cheeks.

'What will happen to us now?' she asked.

'Nothing that hasn't happened somewhere else already,'
he said.

'But nothing like this ever happened in Leaca. It's always
so quiet here. Daniel's wife said to me the other day that she
could swoon at times for want of something different.'

'This isn't the kind of difference she meant, I think.'

An hour later the guards came and then the priest and doctor. In the afternoon the body was taken to Sligo for a post mortem. Soon afterwards Sergeant McNally paid Tom Barron a visit. McNally was a big, awkward man, slow in thought and even slower in movement. He removed his cap gingerly so as not to disturb his smoothly combed hair. Placing the cap on the table, he drew a notebook and pencil from his tunic pocket. While Nancy made tea, he got Tom to describe the scene in Canty's kitchen as he recalled it. He said that, as far as he knew, Tom was the last person to talk to the deceased the previous evening. Given the state of the body, the murder must have taken place shortly afterwards. All this was perfectly obvious to Tom. He smothered his impatience and answered the policeman's questions as fully as he could. He had left Paddy in the best of form about half-past eleven. He walked home alone. It was a foggy night. He could barely see past his nose. He did not meet anyone, nor did he notice anything unusual on the way.

'You say you walked home alone. Were you the only person visiting Paddy?'

Tom thought for a moment. It was a question he had not expected to be asked.

'No. A group of us were there earlier.'

'Did Paddy know you were coming?'

'Yes, we had a night's raking, as we say.'

'Did it happen by accident or did someone arrange it?'

'Paddy invited us. He gave us all a drink and we spent the evening chatting like good neighbours.'

'A little party! It must have been something of an occasion. What did you talk about?'

'The lambing and the cold weather, mainly.'

'How many were there?'

'Apart from myself, there was Daniel Burke, Muiris O'Donnell, Marcus Quinn, Cormac Gildea and Neil Durkin.'

'Quite a gathering. Nearly everyone in the townland.'

'I suppose you could say that.'

'Who was missing?'

'Red Miller, he wasn't there.'

'What about the Englishman, what's his name?'

'Nick Ambrose? No, he wasn't there either.'

'It seems to me to have been more of a meeting than a night's raking. Was it to discuss a particular problem?'

Again, Tom hesitated. He wanted to help the sergeant find the killer, but he didn't wish to tell him things that had no bearing on the case. Neither did he wish to be secretive and evasive, in case the sergeant got the wrong impression.

'We've all been losing things around the house, the odd creel of turf, eggs, potatoes, chickens, turnips.'

'I call that larceny. Someone should have told me. It's what I'm here for.'

'It didn't seem that important. Anyway it has nothing to do with what happened to poor Paddy.'

'It may have. You can't be absolutely sure.'

Tom felt impatient and irritated. Quite obviously, the sergeant was determined to get the wrong end of the stick.

'Was there any reason why Red Miller and Ambrose weren't invited?'

'Red Miller and Paddy didn't get on. Something to do with trespassing sheep.'

'And Ambrose?'

'I wouldn't know. Maybe Paddy just forgot to invite him.'

'Has Ambrose ever mentioned losing things?'

'Not as far as I know.'

'Maybe he has less to lose than the rest of you.'

'Maybe.'

'Does that mean you all suspected him?'

'No, it doesn't. We have no idea who's doing it. We decided to be more watchful and try to catch the culprit in the act. But all that's water under the bridge now. It won't help catch poor Paddy's killer.'

'Paddy didn't have enemies. He was murdered for his money. Who do you think could have done it?'

'I thought you'd be telling me, Sergeant.'

'Don't worry, we'll catch him. The law is slow but sure. He won't get away with it, I can assure you. A senior detective will be coming all the way from Sligo tomorrow.'

The Sergeant spent the rest of the day in Leaca. He went from house to house on his three-speed bicycle and questioned everyone he met. Everyone, of course, wanted to know who was under suspicion, but if he had any idea, he wasn't telling. He was a man who liked to invest both himself and the law with the all mystery of majesty. As the schoolmaster put it, what he lacked in genius, he made up for in self-importance.

3

Paddy Canty didn't have a family. There was no one left to look after his animals, and there was no one in the parish to mourn his death except his neighbours. His nearest relation was a nephew who had emigrated to New Zealand eighteen years ago and never returned. Tom Barron was concerned about Paddy's cow and ewes. He spoke to Muiris who promised to call a meeting to discuss what should be done.

'I had a visit from the sergeant,' Muiris said. 'That man couldn't catch his breath let alone a murderer.'

'He came to see me, too.'

'I asked him straight out, "Who's the murderer?" "That's what I aim to find out," he said, brazen as brass. "If you want to know, I'll tell you." That's what I said, not a word of a lie, and, would you believe it, he looked me up and down like I was a simpleton. "All in good time," he said. The way he got up on his bike, you'd think it was a horse.'

'I hope he knows what he's doing,' Tom said.

'You and I know who did it. We all know. The thief is the murderer and the murderer is the thief.'

The meeting was held at Muiris's house. The small kitchen was bright and cosy. Though Muiris was a bachelor who lived alone, he kept the place as spick and span as any housewife. The flagged floor was swept clean and there was a lively turf fire on the hearth, the flames rising to lick the bottom of the black kettle that hung from a sooty pothook.

They found Muiris sitting in the armchair by the kitchen bed, which was screened off by a red curtain that reached to the floor. During the winter months he slept in the kitchen to be near the heat of the fire. In the summer he slept in the lower bedroom, where the bed was longer and wider and more comfortable.

'We'll have a drink first,' he said when the kettle had boiled.

He placed five small glasses in a row on the table and filled them to the lip with clear liquor from a bottle without a label. Then he got a bottle of Jameson and a larger glass, which he half-filled with whiskey and topped up with hot water from the kettle. He dropped two cloves from a paper bag into the glass and stirred in a spoonful of sugar. Finally, he gave one of the small glasses to each of them and kept the hot toddy in the large glass for himself.

'Neat poteen gives me terrible heartburn,' he explained, raising his tumbler. 'Here's to Paddy, may God be good to him. We may complain about the weather, but, when all is said and done, it's good to be alive. As Paddy himself used to say, "*Nach maith a bheith beo.*"'

They drank to Paddy's memory, and in the silence that followed you could hear for a moment or two the hissing of the fire and the moaning of the wind in the chimney. Muiris smacked his lips as if to lose none of the flavour of either the cloves or the whiskey. From the way he sat in his armchair, you could tell that he considered himself to be in charge of the proceedings. He stretched out his legs and held up his glass against the light. He had a high forehead, a long, thin nose and prominent cheekbones with shadowy hollows underneath. It was the face of a man who knew his own mind and took little note of anyone else's.

'Paddy was a good friend to all of us,' he began. 'We must honour his memory by doing what is right and fitting. First, we must look after his sheep and cow until his nephew comes home, if he ever does.'

They had a long discussion to which each man contributed his pennyworth. Finally, it was decided that they would take turns looking after Paddy's sheep and do their best to make sure that no lambs were lost. Daniel Burke, who had little practice in lambing, said he'd fodder the cow morning and evening instead. The arrangement seemed to satisfy everyone, including Muiris. He got up from his armchair and poured more poteen. This time he didn't make himself a hot whiskey. Instead he knocked out his pipe on the hearth and filled it. Picking up the tongs, he took a coal from the fire and held it over the bowl. It was a ritual they'd all witnessed before, but still they watched as he made loud smacking noises with his lips until the desired amount of smoke began to rise.

'Where would we be without a drink and a smoke?' someone remarked.

'We'd better enjoy them while we can,' Muiris said. 'There may be harp music in heaven but there's no tobacco and no poteen.'

He listened in silence as they made light-hearted conversation about the nature of heavenly pleasures. After a while he shifted his weight in the chair from one buttock to the other, a sure sign of growing impatience.

'Paddy is gone and we're left,' he said. 'The priests talk about the thief in the night but now we've got a more deadly thief to reckon with—a thief of life. It's up to us to make sure he gets the reward he deserves. The Sergeant isn't making much of a shape, so what should honest men do?'

'We must wait and let the law take its course,' Daniel Burke said. 'There's a detective coming from Sligo tomorrow. We must give him all the help we can.'

'The schoolmaster is right,' Tom Barron said. 'We must let the law do its job.'

'Meanwhile there's a murderer on the loose,' Muiris said. 'Has any of you thought of that?'

'We'll have to be careful and bolt the door every night before going to bed,' Cormac said.

'Like Paddy, we're all past our best. He was no match for that young bugger,' Muiris reminded them.

'Paddy wasn't expecting trouble,' Tom said. 'Now the rest of us have been warned, we won't do anything foolish.'

Muiris was not impressed by their lack of purpose. He asked if anyone knew whether Paddy had kept much money in the house.

'Paddy was like the rest of us. He had no reason to lose sleep over his few coppers,' Cormac said.

'Whatever he had, he probably kept in the house,' Muiris reminded them.

'It would be a foolish man who'd kill Paddy for his money,' Daniel said slowly.

'A pound isn't much when you have it in your fist.' Muiris raised a clenched fist as he spoke. 'It's a small fortune if you're without it.' He opened his fist and showed them the empty palm.

'You're right,' Neil Durkin said. 'We must look for a man with a pound to spend, a pound he didn't have yesterday.'

'Only a man with nothing to his name would kill for a pound,' Muiris declared. 'There's only one man in Leaca who fits that description.'

'We're jumping to conclusions,' Daniel reasoned. 'We don't know if Paddy had money in the house and we don't even know if any money was taken.'

'The Sergeant said he found twelve shillings and eleven pence in his jacket pocket,' Tom said. 'The jacket was draped over a chair in the kitchen. If it was money the murderer was after, he'd have taken it.'

'Or he could have made off with the pound notes in the sock under the mattress and left the small change in the jacket to put everyone off the scent,' Muiris said triumphantly.

'How do we know all this?' Daniel Burke asked.

'Schoolmasters want proof of everything,' Muiris told him. 'What proof do we have that there's a God above?'

There was silence in the kitchen for a full minute. The wind drew breath and the fire stopped its hissing. Muiris looked at the six faces before him. The faces were expression-less; they were looking into the fire as if they had not heard.

'I'd advise you all not to leave your money lying around,' Muiris said. 'I've already hidden mine.'

'That won't do much good,' Neil Durkin said soberly. 'There was a story in the paper about an old man in England who was tortured for his money. He was a stubborn old man. He gave up the ghost before he was ready to give up his secret.'

'Well, I've got the right medicine here,' Muiris said, reaching in behind the bed curtains and drawing out a shotgun by the barrel. He patted the stock and stood the weapon against the wall by his elbow. 'That's the lassie will settle him. I oiled her this morning and I'll keep her beside me in the bed every night from now on. If he puts his snout past that door, he'll get the surprise of his life between the eyes.'

One or two of them laughed uncertainly. They all knew Muiris and respected him, but somehow they felt that he was taking things a bit far.

'It's the only gun in Leaca,' Muiris said proudly. 'So far it's only killed crows and foxes.'

'We'll put round the story that you've got a gun at the ready,' Daniel Burke smiled. 'It's one way of making sure you're left alone.'

'There's nothing like a wee companion in the bed on a cold winter night,' Cormac joked.

'Every time you put over your hand, she'll be there,' Marcus Quinn smiled.

'Ye may well laugh while ye can because it's no laughing matter,' Muiris said.

Marcus realised that perhaps he had gone too far in his joshing. They all knew that Muiris was sensitive on the sub-ject of women. 'Sure, we must be saying something,' Marcus said in mollification.

'The man who says something when he should say noth-ing doesn't know the value of words,' Muiris declared.

He refilled their glasses and made himself another hot whiskey.

'I've asked Ambrose to help me with the lambing tomorrow,' he said. 'It's one way of keeping an eye on him. He'll hardly try to murder me in broad daylight.'

'He's a useful man to have around this time of year,' Cormac said. 'None of us is getting any younger. Where would we be without him?'

'We can hire him on day's pay without going soft on him,' Muiris told them. Then he raised his glass against the light of the oil lamp and said, 'To this year's lambs, God bless them.'

4

Nick Ambrose didn't like working for Muiris, but he needed the money. He didn't need a lot of money, but he needed some to encourage Sharon to put off going to Dublin. 'We're down to our last half-crown,' she'd said. 'I'll have to go to Dublin tomorrow unless you earn a few bob today.' Whenever she went to Dublin, she stayed at least a week and came back in a new dress and with more than a pound or two in her pocket. She would stay with her sister, or so she claimed. In truth he didn't know where she stayed, and he thought it best for his peace of mind not to enquire too closely. He couldn't help wondering if all the cash came from the sale of her paintings; he was reluctant to consider how else she could get her hands on the readies so quickly. Her visits to Dublin were a personal defeat that rankled. Besides, he didn't like having to cook for himself and Emily, especially since finding things to cook wasn't all that easy.

Life here was not what you might call a piece of cake. In fact he hadn't tasted cake since he and Sharon left Dublin. Still, he was determined not to complain. He loved Leaca and the people. The spume-showering sea, the wild, untameable landscape, and life pared down to mere essentials, all combined to inspire creativity. It was as if the absence of physical comforts reinforced the springs of imagination and invention. It was such a pity that Sharon could not see Leaca, even for an instant, through his poetic eye.

Sharon never knew her father and mother. She was an illegitimate child who had been adopted at birth by an elderly couple who were childless. They did their best for her, but they both died when she was only fifteen. Her upbringing had taught her self-reliance, and above all it had made her equally suspicious of men and women. Sadly, she had acquired some of the prejudices of the type of ill-begotten Dubliner who sees all country people as 'culchies', in other words, bog-trotters. He had done his best to make her see Muiris and Daniel and the others with an eye of innocence, but she could only associate their faces with physical hardship and the total absence of anything that might bring comfort and support.

His own upbringing in England was little better than Sharon's. His father and mother both drowned while on holiday in Cornwall when he was only three. He was brought up by his Irish grandmother, a wizened old lady who smelt of cloves and lilted him to sleep every evening and whispered unintelligible stories in his ear. He still remembered snatches of her songs and some of the sayings she repeated over and over again, the most memorable of which was, 'Life was nivir like this in Bally-ah-ha.' He couldn't be sure if he'd got the spelling right, but that was what it sounded like on her puckered lips. Snatches of her songs still came to him on the brink of sleep: *Kitty, my love, will you marry me?* and *merrily, cheerily, noiselessly whirring…* something, something, something… *sounds the sweet voice of the young maiden singing.*

When he was ten, his grandmother had a fall from which she never recovered. He was bundled off to live with his Aunt Betty and her husband on a sheep farm on Romney Marsh. They did not think much of his Irish grandmother, and when he was old enough to question them, they pretended to know nothing about her. You could say that he had come to Ireland in search of her, or at least to refresh his memories of her. The first thing he thought he might discover was where she'd come from. He had hoped that 'Bally-ah-ha' would provide a clue, but hundreds of Irish place names began with 'Bally' and 'ah-ha', his version of the Irish *Ath* or *Atha,* was equally common. His grandmother's identity had vanished through one of the gaps of unrecorded history. He looked up records in Dublin, but she did not even qualify for a mention in the short and simple annals of her kind. He gave up hope of ever finding her beloved Bally-ah-ha. He had come to Leaca with a different objective in mind.

Quite simply, he wished to become a writer. When he told Sharon that writing was as important to him as painting was to her, she laughed and said, 'If wishes were horses, we'd all be riders.' The faith she lacked in him, she put in herself. He stared at the whitewashed wall and then at the blank page before him. If only the first sentence would come, the rest would follow like sheep going through a gate.

'I'm going for a walk,' he said. 'I'll be back in an hour or two.'

'Stumped again! Isn't it time you realised that no amount of walking will unstump you?' She laughed at her own easy humour and blew him an ironic kiss for good measure.

He went straight up the hill, head down and arms swinging. He thought he might kill two birds with one stone—look out for some bog oak for the fire while he waited for the all-important sentence to reveal itself. His mind was a patch of proliferating weeds. If only he could grub up the slippery image of Paul Flynn from his thoughts....

When he reached the bogland plateau, he sat on a rock to draw breath. Here, among the perfect geometry of turf stacks, he knew that contentment would finally come to him. Bogs were desolate and mysterious places. The old sites of stacks long vanished resembled the graves of mythological giants from a more romantic era. The thought appealed to him. Somehow it captured the essence of this barren terrain and the imagination of a people bred to hardship and adversity. It was a place that bred truth and purity because here falsehood could find no sustenance. He loved this grey, inhospitable coast pummelled by heavy seas and unruly winds, and he loved the people who had tamed the rocky slopes, fighting for every inch of ground against colonising sedge and rushes.

Rockwell Kent's paintings celebrated the other-worldly atmosphere of this jagged coast. Instead, Nick himself would celebrate its stoical people, men and women who had pared down life to its essentials, who had no truck with either falsity or flimflam.

The relationship from which they drew their strength was their relationship with the land and the sea, every man pulling in time, no man pulling against another, all with the same thought in mind, all bent on reaching the same destination. They helped one another in times of need and shared their meagre possessions whenever it mattered. A good man was not a plausible man but one on whom you could depend in a storm. What was meat and drink to him as a writer was the way they saw each other in terms of stories. Every man's qualities were enshrined in the story that his name evoked. Tom Barron was a man whose word was gospel, Muiris was a man who never gave way, and Red Miller was a penny-pincher who had less need to count pennies than most.

He recalled the story of the day Red Miller went into a pub in Ardara. A stranger came up to him and asked if he knew a man called Red Miller.

'Of course I know him. Wasn't I talking to him only this morning,' Red Miller said in his evasive way.

'Next time you see him, tell him I pulled a ewe of his out of a bog hole the day before yesterday.'

'Don't you know I'll tell him. I'm sure he'll be very pleased.'

The story was told to illustrate Red Miller's meanness. He couldn't bring himself to say who he was and stand the stranger a drink for rescuing his ewe.

Leaca was a place of stories. He would spend his life here if only Sharon could be happy. She was lively and restless; she needed change and excitement. At times he wondered if Paul Flynn was at the back of it all. As Muiris might say, Flynn was the blister on his heel, the pebble in his shoe, and the thorn in the sole of his foot. Or to put it differently, he was the submerged rock in his life, what his neighbours called a *boilg*. *Boilgs* figured strongly in the local imagination because they were a source of danger to men in small boats and must be given a wide berth at all costs. Paul Flynn was such a *boilg*. He would surface in his thoughts at the most unexpected moments, and there was nothing he could do to stop him.

He could hardly think of Sharon without thinking of Flynn. Whenever she came back from Dublin, he would ask her if she'd met him. Invariably, she'd say no, and invariably he'd doubt her word. Flynn was a predator who made no distinction between young prey and old. It was said that he attended men's funerals in order to cosy up to their widows. At one time he'd thought that by coming to Leaca, Sharon would escape his talons, and that he himself might enjoy the luxury of a mind at peace. He could not have been more misguided. Every time she went to Dublin, he couldn't take his mind off Flynn. Sharon loved flattery, and Flynn was master of the flatterer's art. He could flatter while appearing off-hand and matter-of-fact. And he had the knack of implying that anyone who did not agree with him lacked an appreciation of the finer things.

'You come up here a lot. You must be fond of the old bogs.' The voice came from behind. He didn't have to turn his head; he recognised Cormac's drone, which was not unlike that of a didgeridoo.

'I come up here to think,' he said, getting to his feet and facing his neighbour, a small, wiry man with narrow shoulders and sunken cheeks.

'I hope I'm not interrupting.'

'No, of course not. I was thinking that these old bogs look like graveyards. Full of mounds where vanished stacks once stood.'

'It's the men who cut the turf who are in the graveyard. Good men stood where we're standing now. You must be short of turf yourself. I see you've only got half a stack left.'

'It's been a long, cold winter. On my walks I keep an eye out for bog oak for the fire.'

'If it's a *smután* you want, you'll find a good one in my bog. The trouble is getting it out. It's stuck in the gravel and it's nearly twenty feet long. You'll need a pick and a crowbar, and a saw to cut it into lengths you can carry. You can borrow my old pick and you'll get a saw from Muiris. You'll get the crowbar from Tom Barron, I'd say.'

'It's very kind of you. I'm supposed to be working for Muiris tomorrow. I'll borrow your pickaxe the next free day.'

That's what he liked about Leaca. They were all good neighbours together. Even Cormac, who was not his favourite neighbour, was eager to help.

'I'll show you where she's lying,' Cormac said, heading east. He led him to a flat stretch of cut-out bog where the remains of what was once a tree lay flat. After countless millennia it had been exposed in the turf-cutting, and now looked grey and weathered. The branches dug deep into the earth. He could tell immediately that it would be no easy job to dislodge it from its long resting-place.

'You won't mind if I have a go at it?' Ambrose said.

'She's yours for the taking. The man who can raise her deserves her, rump and stump.'

'Thanks a million. The next free day I'll try my luck.'

He said goodbye to Cormac and made for home. He hadn't got his sentence but he'd found enough firewood to last a week. As he reached the lane, Sergeant McNally was cycling up the slope, making heavy weather of the pedalling, veering from side to side on the narrow road.

'I've come up to ask you a few questions, Mr Ambrose,' he said, dismounting.

'I've already told you all I know.'

'All you know or all you want me to know?' He bent down and removed the bicycle clips from the cuffs of his navy-blue trousers. His cheeks an unhealthy red, he looked puffed after the climb.

'What is that supposed to mean?' Ambrose sensed steam rising from under his collar.

'It means that you may have overlooked a vital clue. You must tell me everything, no matter how trivial it may appear to you.'

'Do you want to know what I had for breakfast on the morning of the murder?' Ambrose thought he might try sarcasm.

'It may well be relevant. Let me be the judge of that.'

'I've made a full statement already. I have neither jot nor tittle to add to it.'

'You're very sure of yourself, Mr Ambrose, surer than I am, and surer than Inspector Harper. It was he who suggested that I have another word with you.'

'I could tell you about my bowel movements on the day in question, Sergeant. I took a dose of Glauber salts before going to bed the previous night. I'd been suffering from constipation, you see.'

'Or you could tell me about the young woman who visited Paddy Canty on the fatal day.'

'I know nothing of any young woman except my wife.'

'Then you must be the only man in the townland who didn't see her, but let me refresh your memory. On the afternoon before the murder a young lady in a white car called on Paddy Canty. Everyone in Leaca saw her but no one knows who she was. I'm relying on you to enlighten me.'

'I spent the afternoon fishing from the Leic Chrochta. I didn't see any young woman.'

'Did you meet anyone on the way there or back?'

'Not as far as I remember.'

'How very convenient!'

'What does that mean?'

'If you'd met someone, I might be able to check the accuracy of your story.'

'It isn't a story, Sergeant. Try to understand that.'

'You think you've taken account of everything? Consider it possible that you may be on a sticky wicket. Isn't that what you English call it?'

'Look, Sergeant. I know nothing I haven't already told you.'

'I'll leave you to your thoughts. If ever you'd like to amend your story, you know where to find me. Now I'm going to have a word with Muiris. He's a far-sighted man. He sees more than is visible to your naked eye, for example.'

He felt agitated and angry. The Sergeant had made mush of his peace of mind. His long-sought sentence was still on the other side of the hill.

He had arranged to call on Muiris at nine to help with the lambing. It would be a day of dry bread and short rations, because Muiris, like most of the men around, was no cook. He would have nothing to do with any food that couldn't be got up in less than ten minutes. He could boil eggs and potatoes and make porridge, and very little else. He said that the frying pan had ruined the nation's health; that most food was poison, and that the less you ate of it the longer you'd live.

Unlike Tom Barron, Muiris was not an easy man to work for. He was crusty and devious, a man of hints and nudges. When he spoke, you could never be sure of the meaning he intended. Everything he said was open to several interpretations. You couldn't say he was openly hostile, yet he put paid to any sense of fellowship or community. He made you feel as if you didn't belong. And then again at times he made you wonder if you were imagining it all. Tom Barron, on the other hand, was one of nature's gentlemen. He would share a joke, say what he meant and nothing more, and his wife Nancy was a gifted cook. In fact, he often wished she'd give Sharon a lesson or two in how to make a tasty meal out of next to nothing. He enjoyed working for Tom. He and Nancy were such a happy couple that going to visit them was a pleasure.

He spotted Muiris in the yard in his heavy donkey jacket as he turned into the lane. He was wearing his cold-weather cap complete with earflaps, which had been given to him by a friendly tourist ten years ago. You could tell that he was proud of it. He was in the habit of saying that Shackleton wore one to the Antarctic and that it was the only explorer's hat in the glen.

'Not a bad day for lambing,' Muiris said. 'We'll be all right if it stays dry. The wet and the cold together are the big killers of young lambs. That's what Paddy Canty used to say, poor man.'

'You were one of the last people to talk to him, I hear.' Nick did his best to be friendly.

'Well, apart from the man who murdered him, I suppose.'

'It's a terrible tragedy. He was such a friendly man.'

'He had a great pair of hands for lambing.' Muiris straightened and looked him in the eye. 'He had small hands for a man. That's why he was so good at breech births. He'd have made a great vet if he'd got half a chance.'

'I was with him the morning of the day he died,' Nick said. 'We were gathering in the ewes from the hill.'

'Was that the last time you saw him?' Muiris asked, again looking him in the eye.

'Yes. I left him around noon.'

'Fancy that now. Did you have a bite to eat with him at all?'

'He invited me in for a cup of tea.'

'So you were in his house then the day before the fatal night?'

'I didn't stay long. All we had with our tea was a slice of bread and jam.'

'And wasn't that enough? Most people eat far too much. A healthy man is a thin man, thin as a snipe and hardy with it. As Paddy used to say, the place for the fat is in the fire.'

'It was a strange thing for a peaceable man to say.'

'When Paddy was young, he wasn't peaceable. He'd fight his corner with any man. If the murderer got the better of him in his old age, it was by treachery, not fair play. If I knew who did it, I'd string him up by the heels and flay him from the toes down.'

Ambrose felt distinctly uneasy. Muiris sounded like a man who could lose his temper at any moment. He gave Ambrose a blackthorn and an oilskin bag containing a pair of scissors for cutting the umbilical cords, and a bottle of iodine for rubbing on the navels of the newborn lambs. He himself carried a crook that his grandfather had bought in Inverness as a young man. Ambrose suspected that the crook was like the explorer's hat, part of the personal mythology with which Muiris liked to surround himself. He probably carried it for show or because it was the only shepherd's crook in Leaca. All that was an aspect of Muiris that he didn't quite warm to, though the neighbours seemed to find it engaging. They always said that you could tell what was not in fashion by whatever Muiris was doing and saying.

'It's a bit fresh this morning,' Ambrose said, rubbing his hands.

'Fresh? What do you mean?'

'It's a bit nippy.'

'There must be something wrong with you,' Muiris said. 'You shouldn't feel the cold at your age. I'm over seventy and I don't feel it yet. My only regret is that I never got a chance to go to the Antarctic with Shackleton and experience some real cold. If I'd been with him, he'd have reached the Pole.'

Nick said nothing. He could see that Muiris was in a belligerent mood, and that one careless word could upset the conversational balance.

'We'll go straight up the hill to Log na Seamar and have a look at any new arrivals on the way,' Muiris said. 'Believe it or not, I had the first lamb in Leaca this year and he was black. I'm making out it's a sign of luck.'

'We'll soon find out,' Ambrose said.

'You don't mean it could be bad luck?' Muiris turned and stared at him.

'Well, a black fleece isn't worth as much as a white one.'

'That has nothing to do with luck. Luck gives the most twins and the least deaths in the flock. That's what Paddy Canty used to say. The best year I ever had, I got fifty-nine lambs from thirty-nine ewes, and three of them were black. Now what do you make of your theory?'

'I see what you mean,' Ambrose said, not wishing to encourage Muiris in his desire for combative conversation.

They set off up the hill, picking their steps over the hard ground. The grass was white with frost, which gleamed like tiny pearls in the weak sun. Now and again they stopped on the way to look at ewes that were nearing their time. Some of the ewes were shy, but others didn't seem to mind Muiris and Ambrose feeling their hindquarters. One ewe carried on licking her newborn lamb while Muiris felt her teats to make sure they were clear of wax plugs. He cleaned the mucus from the lamb's nose with a rag while Ambrose applied the iodine to its navel. Another ewe had wandered off by herself and was lying in the lea of a rock about a hundred yards away. She got up and seemed to be pressing, eyeing them both impassively as they approached.

'She's always been a loner,' Muiris said. 'But she won't mind us now. Any other time of year she'd run a mile from you.'

They stood watching the ewe for a while. She was presenting the head and only one foreleg and she was obviously tired. Muiris felt her flanks and belly and bent over her, stroking her neck.

'We'll have to give her a helping hand,' he said. 'You know what needs to be done and your hand is smaller than mine.'

Ambrose took off his jacket and rolled up his shirtsleeves. Though he had done this job several times before, he didn't like having to do it again. It was obvious that the ewe was in pain. Muiris held the hind legs apart and Ambrose put his hand in, slowly and gently feeling his way with his fingers. The other foreleg, which was bent at the knee joint, seemed stuck, and he knew better than to exert too much pressure.

'I'll have to put the head back in,' he said.

'Do what you must do but do it carefully,' Muiris said. 'The poor girl is breathing hard and sweating.'

Muiris was on his knees in what seemed like an attitude of prayer, though praying was not an activity for which he was noted. Now and again he gave a word of advice, speaking quietly as if trying to soothe the poor ewe. At last Ambrose managed to free the foreleg. He breathed a sigh of relief when both forelegs came through with the head in between. After that it was as near to plain sailing as could be expected.

'You're a great girl, so you are,' Muiris said, putting his big hand on her belly. The lamb was slow to start breathing. Ambrose blew into its ears, then slapped it on the ribs, while Muiris tickled its nostrils with a piece of rush. At last the lamb began showing signs of life. The mother got up slowly and began licking the cause of all her anguish.

'He's a fine big fellow, good luck to him,' Muiris said. 'Look at that head and them shoulders. You can almost see the makings of a fine ram in him.'

The lamb was standing with his head down. Muiris lifted him and put his muzzle to one of the mother's teats. Nothing happened at first. Then he began sucking. His tail moved. Within seconds it was wagging with what looked like the purest of pleasure. It was a moment of sheer joy. Ambrose rubbed his hands on the grass and Muiris got out his pipe and lit it.

'It's the first time she needed help,' he said. 'Maybe she's like the rest of us, past her best, or maybe it was the big head and wide shoulders.'

They spent five hours on the hill. They must have walked six or seven miles but Muiris showed no sign of weakening. Ambrose was famished when Muiris finally said that it was time to make for home. On the way back they singled out four heavy ewes and drove them down to the shelter of the paddock by the house where it would be easier to keep an eye on them.

Muiris seemed pleased with the morning's work. He poured Ambrose a generous glass of poteen and drank a bumper of Jameson himself. Ambrose would have preferred the whiskey, but he thought it might be lacking in subtlety to mention it to such a sensitive host.

'I'll eat two eggs,' Muiris said. 'How many will I put on for you?'

'I didn't have one for breakfast, so I'll have three.' He hoped he wasn't pushing his luck.

He watched as Muiris gently lowered five eggs into a saucepan of boiling water. Muiris cut a loaf into thick slices and put half a pound of creamery butter and a pot of blackcurrant jam on the table.

'It's the sign of a good meal,' Muiris said, 'if it takes longer to eat than cook. It will take us twenty minutes to eat this but it only took eight to prepare. What do you think of that?'

'It's the height of efficiency.'

'Sure, there's no sauce like hunger, and no jam like blackcurrant.' Muiris picked up a spoon and topped his egg without wasting any time with preparatory tapping.

'Do you enjoy the lambing?' he asked.

'It's exciting. You never know what's going to happen next.'

'It's my favourite time of year, the spring. It's the only time I feel close to God. Do you believe in God now?'

'Sometimes.'

'And how often is sometimes?'

'Watching a sunrise or a sunset. Or when I'm out alone in a thunderstorm.' Ambrose smiled, but Muiris took no notice.

'Now, isn't that the good one! And here was I thinking Englishmen only believe in themselves.'

'There was an English pope at one time, Adrian IV.' Ambrose thought he might give his host a little surprise.

'But they say the English don't believe in the Blessed Virgin.'

'Some do. There's a shrine to Our Lady in Walsingham.'

'I suppose you believe in the Virgin Queen instead.' Muiris was intent on pursuing his own line of enquiry.

'You mean Elizabeth I? She may have remained a virgin to judge by the paintings of her I've seen, but to tell the truth, I don't really know.'

'Do you think Churchill was a great man of war?' Muiris stared at him as if dying to pick a fight.

'I never voted for him, and I never cared much for his gillie Anthony Eden either.'

'Anthony Eden? Never heard of him. What's he famous for?'

'His headgear. He gave his name to a hat.'

'The man in the hat! Here in Ireland we have the Man in the Cap. Peter McDermott, the left-corner forward for Meath. Hats and caps. I suppose they sum up the difference between the English and the Irish.'

'The best people in England wear caps as well,' Ambrose told him.

Without a word, Muiris got up from the table and made straight for the bedroom. He returned after a few minutes wearing a grey felt hat.

'This hat belonged to my father. He left it to me when he died, and I never wore it till now.'

'It's a good hat,' Ambrose said. 'I think you should wear it with the leaf pulled down in front.'

Muiris adjusted the hat and walked to the door and back.

'I think I'll wear it to Mass next Sunday,' he said.

'It suits you, you know, and it makes you look taller.'

'I'm tall enough already, so I am.' Muiris laid the hat on a chair and returned to the table. He buttered a slice of bread and covered the butter with blackcurrant jam.

'I'll bet it's an Anthony Eden hat,' he said after a while.

'I don't think so, somehow.'

'My father knew about hats. He wore nothing but the best.'

'Anthony Eden's hat was black.'

'Grey, black, what does it matter? A hat is a hat, and the man who wears it is a man in a hat.'

Muiris suddenly rose from the table, as if deeply offended. 'That took me ten minutes,' he said. 'You stay as you are. I see you can't eat and think at the same time.'

He went and sat in his armchair by the fire. Within two minutes he'd reamed, filled, and lit his pipe. Ambrose felt like telling him that he was a time-and-motion man's dream, but he didn't. He was inclined to the view that in certain situations the least said the better.

'You'll come and help me again tomorrow?' Muiris said when Ambrose had finished eating.

'I'll come the day after tomorrow. I've promised to help Daniel tomorrow.'

'But he has no sheep!'

'He's building a turf shed. He asked me to help him make blocks.'

'The blocks can wait but my ewes won't. You know yourself how it is with ewes.'

Nick was reluctant to disappoint him. At the same time he didn't want to pass up an opportunity to have dinner with the schoolmaster, if only because his wife could cook.

'I'll come to you in the morning and I'll help Daniel in the afternoon. How's that?'

'All right, but come early. We'll start at eight and I'll pay you for both days tomorrow.'

'I'm afraid I need the money now.'

'I'll pay you for today, then. And I'll pay you for tomorrow when the morrow comes.'

'That's fine,' Ambrose said, taking the two half-crowns that Muiris offered.

He felt relieved that the ordeal was over. He didn't know what to make of Muiris. He was what was known locally as 'a contrary man'.

5

Daniel Burke put down the local paper as Sheila poured his tea. Ever since he retired over a year ago, he had become more and more aware of time passing slowly. Helping Sheila in the garden and doing odd jobs about the house was hardly enough to assuage the longings of an active mind. In the long nights he read poetry and listened to music on the wireless, but poetry and music weren't everything. What he needed was something in which he could lose himself. Perhaps he should try to write something himself, but sixty-six was rather late in the day to start.

He had spent his working life teaching in the local school, apart from two years in a school in north Dublin. He didn't like the city. He yearned for the country and long evenings fishing after school closed at three. Almost inevitably, he married Sheila, a local girl whom he'd known since boyhood. It was a happy marriage, and it would have been even happier if they'd been blessed with children. From habit they now did everything together. They devoted their lives totally to each other. There had never been anyone else to amuse or distract. They had weathered no great storms. They could both look back on a calm sea and reasonably prosperous voyage. It was only now towards the end that he felt they had missed out on life's great adventure.

The thought came to him last summer on their first holiday on the continent. At the end of a week in Rome they visited the Sistine Chapel for the second time. He looked up at Adam and Eve slinking out of the Garden of Eden and knew that he had wasted his life. It was a feeling that pursued him all the way home and continued to rise like an intrusive outcrop to vex and distract at odd moments of the day and night. He could not mention it to Sheila, of course. Instead he thought up little projects for himself. The new turf shed, he realised, was one of these.

'Ambrose will be coming in the afternoon.' He looked up as he stirred his tea.

'I suppose he'll expect to eat with us,' Sheila said.

'I suppose he will.'

'I don't care for him very much. There's something about him that isn't altogether wholesome.' She'd always been difficult to please in men. To be fair, she was equally critical of women.

'He's good with his hands, and he knows more about block-making than I do.'

'I suppose I'll have to put up with him, then,' she said.

He himself wasn't overfond of Ambrose either, and not just because he was a newcomer in the townland. Somehow he didn't behave like an Englishman, or anyone's idea of how an Englishman might behave. English people, he knew from his reading, were self-reliant. They minded their own business and kept their own counsel. By instinct they were conservative. If anything, they were over concerned about doing the right thing. From the start Ambrose seemed to enjoy makeshift living. He saw himself as an artist, gloriously untrammelled by the conventions that bound the neighbours he'd left behind in England. At least that was the impression he sought to give. He and Sharon had come to Leaca to experience something of what they called 'Neolithic living' before it was too late. In their attitudes they themselves seemed anything but Neolithic. They had the look of city people, they talked like city people, and they knew how to get the most out of their neighbours.

Ambrose was keen to make friends. He saw himself as a citizen of the world, equally at home in London, Paris and

Timbuktu. He was pushy and insinuating. He assumed that he was one of the locals just because they stopped to speak whenever they met him on the road. As Daniel well knew, you could live in Leaca for five generations without being accepted by the likes of Muiris, who saw himself as 'an old residenter' in contrast to all mere residents. Muiris was never done talking about *sean stoc Leaca,* the old stock of Leaca. Now that Paddy Canty had gone, he saw himself as the last of the breed. Needless to say, he saw Ambrose and Sharon as spindrift blown in on the wind.

Ambrose was in the habit of borrowing books from Daniel, and more often than not he had to be reminded to return them. He was also in the habit of giving him poems and short stories for his comments. The poems were senti-mental and self-indulgent, and the short stories shapeless. So far he had not had anything published, but non-publication did not deter him from writing. Daniel read his efforts with some reluctance. Though Ambrose demanded what he called 'an honest appraisal', what he really expected was unstinting admiration. At the slightest hint of criticism he would say that the author's intentions had been misunderstood. Only he knew what these were, and only the most attentive reader would ever discover them.

'I'll be happy if he doesn't bring me yet another of his poems,' Daniel said.

'You're far too easygoing. You should tell him you can't read his writing, and that he should save his stories till they're printed in book form.'

Ambrose arrived at two in the afternoon carrying a large brown envelope.

'I fear the worst,' Sheila said when she saw him coming up the lane. 'That envelope is big enough to hold the *Iliad,* the *Odyssey* and the *Aeneid* all together.'

'*Dia sa teach,*' Ambrose said from the door. It was one of the many irritating things about him, his attempts at the Irish phrases he'd picked up from the neighbours.

'Come on in,' Daniel said.

'Something that came back in the post this morning.' He handed Daniel the envelope. 'Maybe you'd have a look at it and see if you agree with the publisher.'

'I'm reading *Crime and Punishment* at the moment,' Daniel said, by way of discouragement.

'Lucky man. I'm too busy writing to have time to read anything.'

Daniel took the proffered envelope and laid it on the table. 'I suppose we'd better make a start while the afternoon is still young,' he said.

He had lifted gravel from the river and had bought two bags of cement in Melvin's. He had borrowed moulds from Tom Barron and an extra shovel from Muiris. To give him his due, Ambrose put his back into mixing and tamping the concrete. He was stronger than Daniel, and once he got going he was happy to keep at it. They worked doggedly throughout the afternoon, pausing only for a cup of tea at five. Ambrose was preoccupied. For a long time he didn't say anything. The only sound he uttered was an occasional grunt.

'I'll be glad when this investigation is over and the culprit arrested,' Daniel said as they tamped the last of the concrete. 'It's a terrible nuisance. I never bolted my door before going to bed until now.'

'I don't have a bolt on mine, just a latch and nothing else.'

'None of us will sleep soundly till the culprit is caught.'

'Who do you think did it?' Ambrose asked.

'Like everyone else, I'm hoping the Sergeant and Inspector Harper will find out.'

'They interviewed me for over an hour, asking the same questions over and over again, as if they suspected I was spinning them yarns.'

'They questioned everyone in Leaca.'

'But not for over an hour!'

'It's their job to suspect everyone and leave no stone unturned.'

'Someone must have told the Sergeant something against me,' Ambrose said. 'He had the air of a man who thought I had something to hide.'

'He knows that someone does, I suppose.'

'But you don't think I'm guilty.'

'Well, of course not. Every man is innocent till found guilty by judge and jury.'

'If only everyone thought as you do. People look at me on the road as if I were an impostor. "Blame the blow-in" written on every face.'

'I think you're being oversensitive, imagining things that aren't there.'

'I wish I hadn't gone to help Canty that morning. The florin he paid me was dearly bought. The Sergeant kept asking me about it. He thinks I found out where Canty kept his money. I kept telling him he took the coin from his hip pocket but it didn't seem to register.'

'He asked us all the same questions. He even questioned Tom Barron, Paddy Canty's closest friend.'

'Maybe I am too sensitive. It's the price I pay for being a writer. Still, I'd like you to know I didn't do it.'

'And I'd like you to know that I didn't do it.'

Ambrose looked at him. 'Perhaps you're right,' he said, brightening.

Dusk was already gathering when they downed tools. Between them they had made sixty-one blocks.

'There's nothing more we can do now except leave them to cure,' Ambrose said.

'We can have dinner in the meantime.' Daniel led the way into the house.

Sheila had prepared a rich lamb stew with turnips and carrots mashed together. Ambrose was hungry. He ate everything she set before him and didn't say no to a second helping. He ate purposefully and in silence. It was only when they had finished that he asked Daniel if he had read his poem. For a moment Daniel was at a loss. Ambrose was in the habit of giving him at least half a dozen poems a week.

'Which one do you mean?' he asked.

'The one that begins, "Today I asked a stone a question."'

'I thought it derivative,' Daniel said. 'I remember once reading a poem in Irish that began with the same statement.'

'You must admit that it's arresting.'

'But it isn't original.'

'I don't know a word of Irish poetry. If it already occurs in Irish, it only shows I'm on the right track.'

'I suppose you could call it uncanny,' Daniel said.

Ambrose laughed appreciatively. 'You're right there,' he said. 'And isn't that why they won't publish me? They're scared, you see.'

'Scared of what?'

'Of an Englishman who can write more Irish than the Irish. I'm thinking of adopting an Irish pen name, just to fox them. I've had sixty-two rejection slips since I started writing. I'm hoping "Peadar Mac Grianna" will do the trick.'

Sheila offered him more tea to unseat him from his hobby-horse, but Ambrose was not to be thrown. It was not until Daniel said that he was looking forward to making a start on his latest work that he rose to go.

'I mustn't keep you from your pleasure,' he said. 'You're my only reader and critic. Who knows, one day you may be famous.'

'I think he's mad,' Sheila said when he'd gone. 'Is he mad enough to kill for money? That's what I'd like to know.'

'He may be a nuisance but he's harmless,' Daniel said.

'*Today I asked a stone a question.* It may be good poetry in Irish but I doubt if ten professors could convince me it's good poetry in English.'

6

*R*ed Miller was mending the fence that had caused the trouble between himself and Paddy Canty. To judge by the look on Canty's face when he saw the damage, you'd think it was the boundary of hell itself that had been breached. Canty was impossible, even at the best of times. He saw everyone under seventy as a stripling. He himself was above the law, of course, since he happened to be the oldest man in Leaca. No wonder Canty and Muiris Mór got on so well. They were two of a kind.

Still, it was unfortunate that he and Canty had had words, and even more unfortunate that the Sergeant had got wind of it. From the very beginning, he could tell where the Sergeant's questions were leading. And then there was that detective bloke from Sligo. Inspector Harper, he called himself. He was worse than the Sergeant. It was obvious he'd been trained not to believe a word he was told. So where did the Sergeant and Harper get their information? From Muiris, who else?

Muiris was another impossible neighbour. Always going on about the O'Donnells and the old Irish aristocracy of Donegal. Naturally, he saw himself as one of them. He claimed direct descent from Red Hugh O'Donnell on his father's side, and on his mother's side direct descent from Colmcille. All baloney, as everyone knew, everyone except Muiris.

It was laughable how he tried to behave like an aristocrat, or as he imagined an aristocrat might behave. One sports night he and Red Miller were drinking in Cashel. It was a warm evening and the pub was crowded, when suddenly everyone looked suspiciously at the man next to him. Red Miller looked at Muiris, and Muiris looked at Red Miller. 'Was that you, Muiris?' Red Miller asked. Muiris drew himself up to his full height of six foot four and sniffed magisterially. 'It's over twenty-three years since I last farted,' he said seriously. Red Miller felt like saying, 'It must have been a good one,' but he didn't. Muiris was not a man to take a joke.

In his prime he was said to be the strongest man in the parish. One evening when a group of men were standing outside Jamie Byrne's shop talking about cod fishing, a man from the Bachta made a slighting remark about fishermen that didn't go down well with Muiris. Putting out his big hand and placing it on the crown of the shorter man's head, he slowly turned the head so that it was looking over its owner's shoulder. He pressed down on the crown, gently at first and then with all his might. The man's legs gave way beneath him and he sank to his knees on the pavement. Muiris held the man down without losing the thread of his conversation. Only when the man said, 'Sorry, Muiris, I didn't mean it,' did he release his grip. The man got to his feet and staggered off down the street as if drunk, though everyone knew he was a teetotaller. Muiris kept up his conversation with the other men, as if completely unaware of the strength that had gone out of him. The following day he was the talk of the glen. No one ever dared cross him again. Red Miller was only a lad at the time. He saw it happen with his own two eyes.

He'd been watching the Sergeant pedalling up the brae long before the Sergeant spotted him. Dismounting with obvious care, he laid the bicycle against the pier of the gate.

'I've got bad news for you. I've been instructed to arrest you and take you to the barracks for further questioning.'

'You can question me here,' Red Miller said.

'It's out of my hands. I'm only acting on Inspector Harper's orders.'

'How long will the questioning take?'

'That depends on your answers. You could be held overnight or even longer.'

'You must be crazy. You know I didn't do it.'

The Sergeant thrust out his chest and then his chin. 'If you don't come willingly, I'll have to take appropriate measures,' he said.

'I can't leave my ewes in the middle of lambing. Surely you must know that.'

'The law, like the tide, waits for neither man nor ewe.'

'Give me time to get someone to look after my sheep and cattle. When that's done, I'll come to the barracks on my own. I don't need an escort. You'll be the laughing stock of the parish, Sergeant. I'm as innocent as that newborn lamb there.'

'I'll give you till six o'clock this evening,' the Sergeant said, going back to his bicycle.

Red Miller stood watching as he freewheeled down the Ard Breac. He would have to tell Tom Barron about his problem. Tom was reliable. He would know what to do.

When Tom Barron told Nancy that he was going to another meeting at Muiris Mór's, she asked if Muiris was the only man in the townland who could think for himself. She would never understand why Muiris had such influence over other men. There was nothing special about him except his height and vanity. Whenever he called a meeting, the other men came trotting. Of course, no woman was ever invited. The meetings were always held at the house of a bachelor or widower, so that the men could drink poteen together and pretend to be important. Tom was as bad as the rest of them when it came to Muiris. He would listen to Muiris when he wouldn't pay attention to anyone else. It was his only fault. He was solid and sensible in every other way.

'What's the meeting about?' she asked.

'Red Miller. He asked me to look after his ewes and lambs while he's in custody.'

'You don't need a meeting for that, do you?'

'I need help. I've got my own sheep to look after.'

'You won't get much help from Muiris, surely?'

'We'll have to take it in turns. We're all in the same boat, short of help. If anything happened to me, I'd expect the neighbours to lend you a hand. Miller may not be everyone's idea of a good neighbour but his sheep are like everyone else's.'

He took his hat from its peg and put it on in front of the mirror, adjusting it carefully so that it looked as if it had been put on casually. From the window she watched him go down the lane in the gathering dusk. He was a bit of a dandy, was Tom. He always got her to polish his shoes for Mass on Sunday and had her brush the shoulders of his jacket before he left the house. He and Muiris were the only men in the townland who wore a hat on Sunday. All the others wore peaked caps. Tom bought his first hat as soon as they got married, a grey felt hat with a silk band and white silk lining. She always thought he looked good in a hat. Somehow it suited the shape of his face, and when he wore it with his tweed overcoat in winter, she would tell him that he looked like Joe Rooney, the Fianna Fail TD. Naturally, that would please him, though he'd be sure to say that Rooney was good for nothing but shouting his head off on public platforms.

Muiris on the other hand looked like the devil himself in a hat. He had a long body and a long thin face and his hat looked as if someone had hung it on a stick. She couldn't say which of them started wearing a hat first. Probably Tom. More than likely Muiris started wearing one so as not to be outdone. Muiris was deep. Whenever he met her on the road he would raise his hat, but he wouldn't stop to talk unless she started a conversation first. Then he would look out over her head as if he was addressing the mountain behind her. He wouldn't smile, not even with his eyes, and he would end the conversation when it suited him by saying, 'Sure, we must be saying something to pass the time.' He would never forgive her. More than likely he hadn't forgiven Tom either. He was quite capable of trying to get even.

She was pleased that Jim was coming home next month to help with the cutting of the turf. She took his letter from behind the clock and put on her spectacles. She liked reading his letters, because his handwriting resembled her own and because he could twist an expression to make her laugh. For a journalist he wrote short letters. When she asked him why he didn't write longer, he said that he was so used to writing for money that he had forgotten how to write for pleasure. He never wrote to his father, always to her, but he would be sure to mention him. Sometimes he would enclose a fiver for her to spend on herself, but she always bought something sensible for the house. She was proud of Jim. As a boy, he was good at farm work and good at his books. He could turn his hand to anything. She wasn't surprised when he won a scholarship, but she was disappointed when he became a journalist. Somehow she had expected him to do something more useful, something a bit more solid. He was still young, of course, only thirty-six. There was no knowing what he'd turn to next. She had written to tell him about Paddy Canty's death, and she'd sent him the cutting from the local paper. He was friendly with Paddy. He had been making a collection of his old stories, what he called the *seanchas.* He always spent time with him whenever he came home. He had written an article about him for the *Irish News,* and he was writing a book about Leaca in his spare time because, he said, it was a way of life that would vanish with the old generation. He was right there. The young people had gone. Soon the place would be left to the crows and foxes. Having folded Jim's letter and put it back in its envelope, she lit the oil lamp, took a pen and notepad from the mantelpiece and sat down at the table. Jim was bound to be interested in the latest news about Red Miller.

Tom would have preferred not to involve Muiris in his negotiations, but that would be risking trouble. If he made his own arrangements with the other men, Muiris would be offended. They wouldn't fall out exactly, but he would sense a distinct chill in the air whenever they met. It would be the equivalent of what the schoolmaster called 'a serious diplomatic incident'. Everyone in Leaca knew Muiris's little vagaries. Years ago people feared his physical prowess. Now that he was old, they feared the sting of his tongue. Tom knew him better than anyone and had better reason than most to tread carefully in his dealings with him.

Their relationship went back a long way. As young men they played football for the local GAA club. They played midfield and between them they controlled the game. If one of them wasn't in the right place, the other was sure to be. People said that each must know instinctively what the other was thinking. All went well till they both fell in love with Nancy Gallagher, a near neighbour. Muiris was not a man to dally.

He said to Tom, 'I'm going to ask Nancy to marry me.'

Tom thought for a moment. 'So am I,' he said.

'I was first to say it,' Muiris insisted.

'But I was first to think of it,' Tom told him.

'We'll put it to a trial of strength,' Muiris said, knowing that he was taller and stronger than his friend.

'No, we won't. It's up to Nancy to decide for herself.'

'Coward,' Muiris said.

'I'm not a coward. If you like, we'll see which of us can swim fastest and farthest without resting,' Tom said, knowing that he was the better swimmer.

'I know what we'll do,' Muiris said. 'We'll both ask her out for a walk tomorrow evening, and we'll both put the question at the same time. That way neither of us will have an unfair advantage.'

'That suits me,' Tom said.

Muiris didn't keep his word. He went straight to Nancy and asked her to marry him. Nancy said that she wasn't ready to marry anyone, but when Tom asked her the following evening, she said yes. Muiris cried, 'Foul!' He accused Nancy of double-dealing, and Tom of going behind his back, and he refused to have anything further to do with either of them. He stopped going to dances and 'big nights', and when Tom and Nancy got married he refused to come to the wedding. It was eleven years before he and Tom exchanged a friendly word again, and even then their relationship was far from easy. There was no delight in their conversation because Tom had to be careful not to offend him again. Nancy said they were worse than schoolboys. She accused Tom of paying too much attention to Muiris. The truth of the matter was that Tom needed to be on good terms with him. The years when they weren't talking were the most dismal of his life.

'We thought you'd forgotten us,' Muiris said as Tom opened the door.

The other neighbours were already gathered and Muiris was pouring poteen. When they'd all had a swig, Tom told them what Red Miller had asked him to do. Muiris said that it would be unfair to expect Tom to look after Miller's sheep on his own. In a long discussion in which every man had his say, they all agreed to give a helping hand. Muiris worked out a rota so that no man would have to do more than his neighbour. For a moment nothing further was said. Then Muiris posed the question that was on everyone's mind.

'Is Red Miller really guilty?' he asked. 'I don't think he is.'

'I don't think so either,' Cormac said.

'Miller's an awkward customer but he's no murderer,' Marcus Quinn put in.

'If he isn't guilty, then the murderer is still at large,' Muiris said. 'Think of that.'

'We'll not be safe in our beds at night till the real culprit is caught,' Marcus Quinn agreed.

'But who is the real culprit?' Muiris asked.

'Nick Ambrose, who else?' Cormac said.

'What must we do about him, then?' Muiris looked at each man in turn.

'It isn't for us to decide,' Daniel Burke said.

'We all know what the Sergeant is like,' said Cormac.

'That man can't see past his nose,' his friend Marcus agreed.

'If there's no evidence against Miller, he won't be charged,' Tom Barron said. 'Then the real murderer will be arrested.'

'And valuable time will be lost.' Muiris brought down his right fist on the palm of his left hand.

'We must do something,' Cormac said.

'We're not the law.' The schoolmaster shook his head in disbelief.

'I'll go to the Sergeant and tell him what we think,' Muiris said.

'Now you're talking,' Cormac agreed. 'Tell him about Nick Ambrose and ask why he hasn't been arrested.'

'I won't tell him how to do his job, not in so many words, but I'll make him think again, so I will. What do you say, Tom?'

'I suppose there's no harm in trying,' Tom said.

'I think you're all very wrong,' Daniel cut in. 'You're trying to interfere with the natural course of justice.'

'We're oiling the wheels of justice,' Muiris said. 'Now that we've come to a decision, I think we all deserve another drink.'

'I'll tell you a good one while you're pouring,' Cormac said. 'Who did I meet on the hill the other day but my bold Ambrose. Sitting on a stone, he was, eyeing Tom's turf stacks, and I'd swear on the book that he was thinking of pinching a creelful. I thought I'd make him work for his firing, so I told him about the big heavy *smután* that's half-buried in my bog. Well, would you believe it, he fell for it. He'll lose some sweat before he gets that one home, let me tell you. It failed my father to shift her, and my father was a dogged man.'

'Maybe we should give him a hand,' Daniel said seriously.

'It would be a waste of time,' Cormac told him. 'That tree will lie where it fell. The heartwood's as hard as iron. There's not a saw in the county that would cut through it.'

Cormac laughed and so did Marcus.

'It isn't funny,' Daniel said. 'Leading an innocent stranger up the garden path.'

'Innocent?' Cormac laughed.

'You should save your sympathy for a better cause, Daniel. That bucko is well able to look after himself.' Muiris spoke with an upward tilt of the chin.

They talked about the lambing for a while, and there was general satisfaction when Daniel said that the radio had forecast good weather for the coming week. After a while Daniel took a page of the *Irish News* from his jacket pocket and held it up for them to see. As the only man in Leaca who took a daily newspaper, he was the local expert on what was going on in the world, a position of which he was justly proud.

'It's an article by Jim Barron,' he said. 'If I know anything, it will make people think.'

'Read it to us,' Muiris said. 'Then we'll all know what you mean by "think".'

They listened in silence as Daniel read the article. It was a long article describing the effect the murder was having on an isolated and law-abiding community in which serious crime was hitherto unknown. It spoke of fear and suspicion and the failure of the police to ensure people's safety. As Tom listened to the schoolmaster's even intonation, he couldn't help wondering where Jim had got his information. It was as if he had been living among them and privy to their innermost thoughts. Truly, he thought, journalists had a sixth sense. It was strange to think that Jim was his and Nancy's son.

'Read us the bit about Inspector Harper again,' Muiris said when Daniel had finished.

'"Inspector Harper told your correspondent that the deceased had died of cardiac arrest brought on by the shock of the attack. It was likely, therefore, that the culprit, when caught, could not be charged with murder since the victim had died of natural causes. A full team of investigators had been assigned to the case because of its seriousness. Inspector

Harper appealed to people living alone not to leave large sums of cash in their homes. He said the motive for the attack was robbery, and described it as an act of gratuitous barbarity. The *gardaí* were investigating several leads at once, among them the possibility that a heavy motorcycle heard passing through Carrick at 3.30 a.m. on the night of the murder may have been connected with the crime."'

'Motorcycle, my arse,' Muiris said. 'Did you ever hear anything so stupid?'

'If there was a motorbike, why didn't any of us hear it?' Cormac said.

'And it wouldn't have gone through Carrick, now would it?' Marcus agreed with his friend.

'The man who said Paddy died of natural causes is a fool,' Cormac declared. 'Paddy was murdered, and if he hadn't been murdered, he'd have lived another ten years. He was as hardy as a snipe and as healthy as a trout, so he was.'

'The guards don't know what they're doing,' Muiris said. 'If we don't do something soon, they'll let the murderer slip through their fingers.'

'There's nothing we can do but wait.' Tom Barron shook his head.

'I'll go to the Sergeant tomorrow and let him know what we all think,' Muiris said.

In the morning he got Daniel to drive him to the barracks to save valuable lambing time, as he put it. Four hours later Red Miller was released for lack of evidence. Muiris attributed this development entirely to his own intervention.

When he heard the news, he said to Tom Barron, 'What did I tell you? I should have been a detective. Mark my words, Ambrose will be arrested before the week is out.'

7

*H*e was sitting at the kitchen table, waiting for the ending of a short story to reveal itself. This particular story had imprisoned his mind and heart for two whole weeks, and still it had not declared its final shape. It was a story about a patriarchal figure, an inglorious Irish Moses, who dominated the life and thoughts of every one of his neighbours.

The bleat of a ewe roused him from his reverie. She was standing on the bank outside the back window looking in at him. For a moment she seemed to nod in recognition. Then with another plaintive bleat, she was gone. Would her bleat serve as a covert authorial comment on the ramblings of the unreliable narrator of his story? For a moment he sensed that at last he had found his ending. After all, to misquote the Bard, the best in this kind are but accidents. He wrote down the sentence in pencil and sighed as he struck it out again. He would recognise the true ending, the only ending, when it finally came.

The patriarch in his story reminded him of Muiris, one of those men who do not know the meaning of uncertainty. Muiris was firmly convinced that he knew instinctively what was good for his neighbours, which happily coincided with his idea of what was good for himself. He had wasted his life, of course, languishing here in the obscurity of Leaca instead of enjoying the life of a colourful king in some remote Pacific island of the nineteenth century, indulging his lust for power and every imaginable fleshly appetite.

In his story he had been at pains to convey, however obliquely, something of the dark and unknowable side of life in Leaca—what Muiris referred to as 'the stench of warm blood in the air even on the coldest day'. It wasn't the blood of lambing, which he could wash off his hands after a morning on the hill. This was the kind of stench that Muiris called a *dachtán,* a stench that rose from the earth itself, a heavy reek of decay and decomposition that only strong men could stomach. Muiris said that the Irish soil was soaked in Irish blood; the blood of ancient gods, martyrs, heroes. You could get it cutting turf in summer or digging wet or heavy clay, the smell of the rotting innards of the earth itself.

'It reminds me of gutting an old hen, or gutting a fish that isn't fresh,' Muiris had said. 'The ground we stand on is rotting beneath our feet. It's rotting even as we speak.'

Ambrose had never experienced any of this. He wondered if Muiris was pulling his leg or trying to bamboozle him into thinking his own primitive thoughts. Tom Barron and the other men never spoke of this *dachtán*. He'd check with Daniel, who had a scholarly knowledge of the Irish language and Irish history, and whose opinion was objective and not to be dismissed lightly.

If only he had a study like Daniel's, or even a den where he could be alone at a desk facing a blank wall with no sound reaching the ear except the cry of a gull or a dog's far-off bark. Unfortunately, Sharon was a talker. She never seemed to run out of things to say. Like him, Emily was happy to be silent. She was more self-reliant than any child he'd ever known. Already she could look after herself, more or less, and she did not seem to mind being left alone.

He enjoyed taking her for walks on the cliffs and along the shore. She was intelligent and alert. She would ask him one question after another, questions that even he could not answer. One day he pointed to a hovering hawk and told her that it killed and ate little birds like robins and thrushes.

'Did God make the hawk?' she asked. He thought for a moment and said yes because it seemed the truest answer.

After a moment's silence she asked if God hated robins and thrushes. When he told her that he didn't know, she said that Mummy knew more than he did. Mummy had told her that God made the hawk to kill songbirds because they woke Him up with their singing too early in the morning.

He looked at Sharon, who had just finished combing Emily's hair. At times he did not know what to make of her. He would never get to know her. What went on in her head was a mystery that no amount of scientific investigation would reveal. Perhaps that was why he could not conceive of a life without her. He put the thought from his mind and tried to concentrate on his story, but it was no good. It was to be one of those blank and dreary days.

'I'm going for a walk,' he said, closing the sixpenny jotter.

'And what do you expect to find on your travels?' She spoke without raising her head.

'An ending for my short story.'

'A lost shilling would be more useful. We're down to our last half-crown again.'

'I'm due to work for Tom Barron tomorrow.'

'Another five shillings won't get us very far. You must know perfectly well that this can't go on.'

'We didn't come here to live in luxury. We came, if I remember correctly, to live the simple life. Plain living and high thinking. It was your friend Paul Flynn who suggested it.'

'This isn't living, it isn't even partly living.'

'I've never been more creative. I get new ideas every day, and so do you.'

'New ideas! Don't kid yourself. Just ask yourself who needs them. You're shitting poetry and short stories without a penny to show for it.'

'You're not doing all that well yourself.'

'Who's the breadwinner, I'd like to know? If I didn't sell a painting every so often, we'd all be on the road by now.'

'I refuse to argue. I'm going for a walk to clear my head of all lumber and baggage.'

'I'll think of you as I try to make lunch from a turnip, five carrots, and six potatoes. It's just as well you're fond of potato cake.'

'If this ground-sea falls, I'll catch a pollock for dinner.'

'In your dreams, you will. Go for your walk and enjoy your navel-gazing. I hope you find more than fluff.'

There was no talking to her. He took his jacket from the peg behind the door and set off up the hill. He wanted to walk and walk, breathing keen air till his brain and blood cooled. He walked briskly with his head down, past places where he and Muiris had delivered lambs only a few days ago. The small mountain ewes had their heads to the ground nibbling short grass, and the lambs were doing their best to extract milk from meagre udders. The scene gave him a sense of rightness, of life flowing naturally, of everything tending in the same direction. The wind that cooled his face ruffled the ewes' fleeces, and the sun that warmed the crown of his head encouraged the lambs to gambol, all of which reinforced his sense of being part of the open world of sky, sun, wind and mountain.

He sat on the crest facing north with his back against a rock, looking down on the business of grazing, gambolling and suckling. It was both business and pleasure, which was how his own, yet-to-be-invented life should be, but alas was not. If only Sharon could see with his eyes… She would go to Dublin again and he would not try to stop her. She would come back, of course. She would never leave him, and neither would he leave her. Each would be incomplete without the other because each of them needed the other as a restraining force, a kind of spancel to ensure their mutual dedication to perfection. It was an odd relationship because more often than not the spancel chafed and made raw, leaving burns and abrasions to be salved and bandaged. Perhaps it was not all that odd. Dogs were known to lick each other's wounds.

His eye turned to the shore and the sea. Rocks from which he had fished on summer evenings now seemed strangely small. The beach of white stones looked no bigger than a postage stamp, the houses little more than bothies. Five empty and eight still inhabited, Tom Barron's at the lower end by the sea and Muiris Mór's at the foot of the hill. They seemed to grow out of the land, fashioned from materials provided by the hill itself. The only extraneous object was the black Ford Anglia parked outside the schoolmaster's door. An unbidden sentence dropped into his mind. The imagination of man's heart is evil from his youth. Was that a clue to the elusive ending of his short story?

He got to his feet with a spang and set off down the slope. His mind was racing, his limbs loose and free. As he came to the disused sheep pen known as Jack's Garden, he realised that he must attend to a call of nature before it was too late. He stood and looked all around. Quickly, he plucked a few handfuls of grass to serve as toilet paper and entered the pen, which consisted of four dry-stone walls with holes between the stones. The wind blew through the holes, making an uncouth sort of whistling. He let down his trousers and allowed his bowels to empty, reminding himself of the schoolmaster's description of the toilet facilities in the local school, 'unlimited expanse of barren mountain'. The phrase, he thought, had a local authenticity, which for the schoolmaster's benefit he would work into his next story. Relieved, he set off down the hill, eager to get back to his writing. He had already reached the road when he noticed the bicycle outside his door.

'Good afternoon.' Sergeant McNally was sitting at the table with his cap resting on his kneecap. 'Can I have a word with you in private, Mr Ambrose?'

'You can have a word with me here. There are no secrets between Sharon and me.'

'There's the little girl,' the Sergeant suggested.

'We don't have secrets from Emily either.'

'I must ask you to come with me to the barracks for further questioning.'

'I've already told you all I know. I can't see what's to be gained by—'

'I'm acting on Inspector Harper's orders.'

'He could have come to interview me here.'

'That is not how the law proceeds, Mr Ambrose. I must warn you that you may be held.'

'This is absurd. I don't know anything I haven't already told you.'

'You haven't told me about the young lady who came to see Paddy Canty on the afternoon before he was murdered.'

'Oh, God, not her again! I've told you I know nothing about her at least twice.'

'I saw her get out of her car,' Sharon said. 'Does that make me guilty?'

'You saw her but your husband didn't!'

'I told you I was fishing at the time!' Ambrose exclaimed.

'And you went fishing because you knew she was coming. For obvious reasons, you didn't want to meet her.'

'He went fishing because the larder was empty,' Sharon said. 'What is more, he caught two pollock. Unfortunately, we had them for dinner, so we can't produce them in evidence.'

'Inspector Harper has a theory that the lady in the car is connected with the murder; that she was working in tandem with someone local.'

'And, of course, that someone must be me,' Ambrose said sarcastically.

'You should tell that to Inspector Harper. I'm sure he'll be interested to hear it.'

'Perhaps I could have a word with Sharon in private.'

'I'll wait outside, but don't be long,' the Sergeant said. 'Both the Inspector and myself are busy men.'

'This is some stupid mistake,' he assured Sharon when the Sergeant had gone out. 'I've had nothing to do with any young woman.'

'What are we to do if you're held in custody?' She put both her hands to her temples.

'We're not entirely friendless. Daniel Burke and Tom Barron will help you out, I'm sure.'

'If you're not back by tomorrow, I'll have to go to Dublin. I'm sure Janice won't mind putting Emily and me up for a while.'

He didn't like hearing the word 'Dublin', but he did not try to talk her out of going. She would have to do what was best for herself and Emily. He picked up Emily and gave her a hug.

'I'll be back soon, darling,' he said, knowing that it was outside his power to promise.

8

*B*ald and hunched, with a left hand that shook uncontrollably whenever he was angry or frustrated, Inspector Harper was not an impressive man to look at, but what he lacked in prepossession he amply made up for in cold decisiveness. Among his colleagues he had acquired a reputation as a skilled interrogator who always knew which questions to ask as well as the most effective order in which to ask them. All things considered, he was not a man to be trifled with.

He motioned to Ambrose to take a seat and told Sergeant McNally that he would call him if he should have need of him. When McNally had left the room, Harper leaned back in his chair and contemplated Ambrose's beard for a good thirty seconds in silence. Ambrose did his best to return his gaze, but he could not help regretting McNally's absence. He knew McNally. Harper was an unknown quantity.

'When did you come to Ireland, Mr Ambrose?' he began.

'Six years ago. In 1942.'

'You came to a neutral country in the middle of the war! That was a strange thing for an Englishman to do. Surely you should have been engaging with the enemy?'

'I served under Wavell in the Middle East for a year and was invalided out of the army.'

'Were you not offered a desk job?'

'I applied for a job with the British Council but I didn't get it.'

'So you came to Ireland instead! Why is it that I find this tale of yours so tall?'

'Perhaps you're a cynic, Inspector. Perhaps you see sophistry and subterfuge where there is none.'

'Why did you come to Ireland?'

'To find out something about my Irish roots. I was brought up by my Irish grandmother in Sussex.'

'What was her maiden name?'

'Quinney. Molly Quinney.'

'And which county did she come from?'

'I don't honestly know. I could find no trace of her in the records.'

'Quinney is not a common name. I don't suppose there are many Quinneys in Ireland.'

'That is also my impression.'

'Did you come to Donegal thinking she might have hailed from here?'

'No, I came to Leaca because the American artist Rockwell Kent lived here for a time in the 1920s. My wife is an artist, you see. Like Kent, we both wished to experience something of the elemental life.'

'Tell me about the young lady who visited Paddy Canty on the afternoon before he was murdered.'

'I know nothing about her. I spent that particular afternoon fishing from a rock called the Leic Chrochta, out of sight of the houses and the road.'

'How convenient! Did you catch anything?'

'Yes. Two good-sized pollock.'

'When did you first hear of the young lady?'

'When Sergeant McNally mentioned her.'

'How very odd! You're the only man in Leaca who missed her. By all accounts she was a great beauty. She seems to have made quite an impression on your neighbours. One man fell for her legs; another for her nylon stockings, which he described as "ankle-tailored by Bradmola". Don't you regret not having seen her?'

'How can I when I know nothing about her?'

'I find that difficult to credit, Mr Ambrose. My theory is that she came to Leaca to spy out the land, to do a recce, you might say. She was in conspiracy with you, the Angel of Death who went before you. Now do you understand?'

'Your theory is preposterous, Inspector.'

'And your story is as full of holes as the young lady's hairnet, Mr Ambrose. Molly Quinney indeed! You must take me for an idiot. Do you see any green in my eye?' He put his forefinger on his left eyebrow and raised the eyelid.

'Quinney was my grandmother's maiden name.'

'Can you prove it?'

'Not here and now.'

'Perhaps Sergeant McNally can help. He knows about family names.'

He went to the door and asked the Sergeant to come in. The Sergeant looked pleased when asked to take a seat.

'Is Quinney an Irish name, Sergeant?' Harper gave him a superior's condescending smile.

'Quinney? Quinn, Quinley and Quinlan are Irish but not Quinney.'

'You're wrong there,' Ambrose said. 'Quinney is an English version of Ó Coinnigh, an old Irish family name derived from that of a sixth-century monk.'

'And I suppose Granny Quinney is your authority for that! Mr Ambrose, your story reeks of fabrication. I think we'll allow you a little time to mull things over and make any adjustments to your tall tale that you may deem advisable. Do we have a room where Mr Ambrose might spend the night, Sergeant?'

'The accommodation here is basic but adequate.'

'This is madness,' Ambrose said.

'It's in your own interest, Mr Ambrose. Think it over. I'll take a statement from you at 9.05 tomorrow morning.'

'What did I tell you?' Muiris said when he heard that Ambrose had been arrested. 'If I hadn't twisted the arm of the law just that wee fraction, the bugger would still be at large.'

'We'll miss Ambrose just the same,' Tom said. 'His help was useful, especially this time of year.'

'We got on without him before he came, and we'll get on without him when he's gone.'

One or two people, including Tom, who'd worked with Ambrose found it difficult to believe that he was a murderer. Nevertheless, there was a general sense of relief that at last everyone could go to sleep at night with an easy mind. There was confusion and disbelief two days later when Ambrose was released without being charged.

A week passed without any further developments. When questioned by Muiris, the Sergeant said that Ambrose was still under suspicion but that the evidence against him was flimsy, at best only circumstantial, and that it would never stand up in a court of law. The Inspector was still making enquiries, which might take some time to resolve. He had a theory that Jim Barron's article about Paddy might have led an outside crook to think that Paddy kept a tidy sum of money in his house. Quite possibly, the young woman who came to see him was on a mission of reconnaissance.

'It's a far-fetched theory,' Muiris sniffed.

'It's the only stone left unturned,' the Sergeant replied. 'Do you have a better idea?'

'I told you what I think. It's as plain as day.'

'We can't hold a man for more than forty-eight hours without charging him.'

'Charge him then.'

'There must be a *prima facie* case against him.'

'Prima fascism, my arse,' Muiris said. 'There's no law in the land.'

That evening Muiris called a meeting, which was attended by all the men of Leaca apart from Ambrose and Red Miller. Muiris poured poteen with noticeable generosity. He gave them a blow-by-blow account of his conversation with the Sergeant and told them that something must be done.

'What can we do?' Neil Durkin asked with an air of innocence.

'We must wait till the guards have finished their investigations,' Daniel said. 'They're still trying to get enough evidence together to make a case that will stand up in court.'

'Ambrose is too cute for them,' Cormac said. 'He's running rings round them.'

'The English made the law,' Marcus Quinn agreed with his friend. 'They all know more about the law than our police.'

'You're right there,' Muiris said. 'I went to school under the English. Old Master McMackin taught us all about Poynings's Law, so I should know.'

'Poynings's Law has nothing to do with it,' the schoolmaster said. 'That was in 1494.'

'I know my history because I've lived through it,' Muiris assured them. 'The laws we have are English laws. The old Brehon Laws are the only laws that matter.'

'I remember my father telling me about them,' Cormac agreed. 'We had Brehon Law in Ireland long before the English had any law.'

'It was blood for blood,' Muiris told them. 'And no prima fascist nonsense.'

'This is wild talk,' Daniel said. 'You know nothing about Brehon Law.'

'I know about the blood fine, and that's enough,' Muiris said.

'Brehon Law was a proper system with a *breitheamh* to give judgment,' Daniel told them.

'But there were no wigs or gowns or fancy collars! That's what's destroying the law,' Muiris said. 'The *breitheamh* was a man in his working clothes like you or me.'

He got up and poured more poteen for his guests, but this time he omitted to pour himself whiskey, saying that he was killed with heartburn and that he'd never eat two rusty mackerel for dinner again.

'The situation is this,' he said, returning to his seat in the corner. 'The guards know that Ambrose is guilty. The Sergeant said as much to me in confidence. "Still under suspicion," those were his very words. We all know what that means.'

'It means that the facts as we know them are not legally sufficient to make a case, and that the investigation is still proceeding,' Daniel said.

'You sound like the Sergeant,' Muiris laughed. 'Only the Sergeant uses the word "proceeding".'

'Muiris is right,' Cormac said. 'If we leave everything in the hands of the guards, nothing will happen and Paddy Canty's murderer will get off scot-free.'

Muiris sat erect in his armchair with the forefinger of each hand in his waistcoat pockets. He surveyed the faces before him one by one. He could have been an old *breitheamh* about to give a weighty judgment in a tricky dispute, the full import of which only he could appreciate.

'You're very quiet, Tom,' he said. 'What do you think?'

'It's too early to say. To tell the truth I find it hard to believe that Nick Ambrose would murder anyone. I've worked with him, and I think I know him. He's a bit odd in his ways but he's harmless. I'd be for giving the police more time.'

'We've all worked with Ambrose and we all get on fine with him,' Muiris said. 'But we must be sensible. He's young and quick. He has a strong pair of hands. I've watched him, believe me. He's the kind of man who doesn't know his own strength. Look at it this way. He knew Paddy had sold his year-old wethers at Ardara fair. He knew he had money on him. He broke into his house hoping for a few pounds and not meaning any great harm. Paddy, like the rest of us, was a light sleeper. He hears a noise in the night and he gets up to investigate. He surprises Ambrose in the dark but Ambrose is too quick for him. He doesn't mean to kill him but in the heat of the moment he goes too far. Paddy is old. His heart isn't what it used to be. In my book it's murder, but the guards and the lawyers will just call it manslaughter.'

'It's murder all right,' Cormac said. 'Isn't that what's wrong with the law? Too many lawyers making silly distinctions.'

'You're right,' Marcus said. 'There's buggery, robbery and larceny, and they all come down to the same thing in the end.'

'I think you must mean burglary,' Muiris said.

'What do you think we should do, then?' Neil Durkin asked.

'I think it must be a life for a life,' Muiris said. 'Paddy was a good neighbour and friend to all of us. We can't just sit here like old women pretending he wasn't murdered. He deserves better.'

'It's easier said than done,' Tom Barron reflected. 'It isn't for us to take a life.' He didn't look at Muiris. He looked into the fire as if he were talking aloud to himself.

'It happened before in our grandfathers' time. We've all heard about Agent Cox and the Triangle.' Muiris looked at his listeners, pausing to allow his words to sink in.

Cox was the landlord's agent in the time of Parnell and Davitt. Over the years he had earned for himself a reputation for stony-hearted brutality and blatant greed. He evicted tenants who were behind with their rent and he increased the rent for anyone who'd made improvements to his house and farm. When he raped a young woman from Leaca two days before she was due to marry, it was the last straw. Her neighbours got together and drew lots to find out who should get rid of him. The next time he came to Leaca, he didn't return. The following day his horse was found ten miles away, at the foot of Slieve League, lame and shoeless with neither saddle nor bridle. There was no sign of Cox, and no one had any idea what could have happened to him. The mountain was searched and the whole coast between Teelin and Maghera, but no trace of a body was ever found.

'I know the spot on the mountain where he's buried,' Cormac said. 'When the sun is low at certain times of the year you can still see the outline of the body in the grass.'

'I never knew that,' Marcus marvelled. 'Next time I'm up there I must look out for it myself.'

'The sun needs to be very low in the sky and the grass needs to be an inch long and you need to jouk down on your hunkers and close one eye.' Cormac closed one eye and looked across at Muiris.

'Our grandfathers knew how to keep a secret,' Muiris said. 'The question is, can we?'

'If we use the Triangle, only one man will know who's the executioner and he's the least likely to tell,' Cormac said.

'Have you all gone mad?' Daniel demanded. 'Don't you realise you're talking about murdering a man who may well be innocent for all we know. Talking and theorising is all very well but actually doing it is something else entirely. Don't you realise that if we get out the Triangle, someone will have to kill him, and it could be you or you or you? Have you thought of that? If you haven't, it's time you did.'

'What if it's you?' Muiris asked.

'I can tell you here and now I wouldn't do it.'

'Nobody is asking you to do it.' Muiris straightened, placing both hands on the arms of his chair as if he were about to spring to his feet. 'No one will be asked to do anything he doesn't agree with.'

'The whole idea is wrong,' Daniel said. 'If Ambrose is charged and found guilty, he'll be given a sentence and he'll be made to serve it. That's the law and that's justice.'

'It's that that's wrong,' Muiris said. 'Paddy Canty wasn't given a sentence and he wasn't let out early on parole either. He wasn't given a choice. He was made to pay with his life. Paddy was a good man, a solid man. He worked hard on sea and land and never owed any man a penny. Compared with him, Ambrose is only road-dust whirling in the wind. He owns nothing, he cares for nothing, and he'll never come to anything. His life isn't worth two sparrow farts.'

'If it's worth even one, he's lucky,' Cormac said.

'You look serious, Tom. What do you think?' Muiris asked.

'It's a serious business. I don't think we should rush into anything. We all need time to think. I would say we need a week to turn it over in our minds.'

'A week it is, then,' Muiris said. 'We'll meet here this night week and come to a final decision. The first question I'll ask every man is this: Are you ready for the Triangle?'

He went round again with the poteen bottle and made a hot whiskey for himself. The conversation turned to less controversial matters such as the weather and the price of springers at Ardara fair. They parted an hour later with nothing but goodwill to all men on their minds.

9

*W*hen Tom got home, it was already past midnight. Nancy had gone to bed but the oil lamp was still burning in the kitchen. He knelt at the armchair and said his night prayers. When he had raked the fire, covering the live coals with ashes, he took off his boots, and got himself a mug of water from the pail by the door. He drank the water and dipped the mug in the pail once more. He always took a mug of water to bed with him because he often woke up parched in the early hours, especially after a glass or two of poteen. The bedroom was in darkness. He took off his shirt and trousers and got into bed in his long johns. He was as quiet in his movements as a mouse because Nancy was a light sleeper and he did not wish to disturb her.

'You stayed out well,' she said, still facing the wall.

He raised himself on his elbow and reached over to kiss her as he always did before going to sleep.

'You smell like a still-house,' she said, turning in the bed.

'Muiris gave us all a glass before we left.'

'What did you do to deserve that? Or should I say, what did he want from you?'

'He's always been good about the poteen.'

'He doesn't drink it himself, I'll bet.'

'It doesn't agree with him. It gives him terrible heart-burn, he says.'

'He knows it rots the mind as well as the gut. It's his way of making sure he'll live longer than the rest of you. What did you talk about?'

'The lambing, the weather, and the price of springers at the last fair.'

'And that took three hours?'

'We talked about a score of other things as well. We even talked about poteen-making for a while.'

'Did you talk about Nick Ambrose?'

'His name came up once or twice. I told them he'll be coming to give me a hand tomorrow.'

'I'll bet Muiris thinks he's guilty.'

'Muiris has his own way of looking at things.'

'Do you think he's guilty?'

'No one knows. Even the guards don't know. They're still casting about for clues.'

'Muiris hates what he calls "blow-ins". A "blow-in" to him is someone whose people weren't in Leaca in the time of Colmcille. By that reckoning, I'm a blow-in.'

'It's nearly one. It's time we got some sleep,' he said.

He knew he wouldn't sleep now. He would lie awake for at least an hour, going over the evening, rehearsing conversations, and making up new ones. His mind was racing but still he settled himself on his back and stretched his arms by his sides. He hoped his legs wouldn't trouble him. Sometimes in bed he got a tingling below the knees that kept him awake. It was a terrible affliction. Doctor O'Rourke called it "restless leg syndrome," but knowing what it was called was no help. The only cure for it was to get up in the middle of the night and walk about for a while till it went away. He listened to Nancy's even breathing and waited patiently with his eyes closed, while his mind wandered aimlessly in a place of shadows.

Nick Ambrose arrived shortly after breakfast. He was wearing an old pair of dungarees and he had a spade on his shoulder like any seasoned workman.

'Not a bad day for fencing,' he said.

'It will have to do,' Tom replied.

They spent half an hour moving the wooden posts and bales of wire netting over to the Barley Field, which Tom used for lambing. There was a dry-stone wall round the field but it wasn't high enough to keep sheep from jumping over it. First, they both inserted the posts at intervals in the wall by removing some of the stones and repositioning them. Then they stretched the wire netting and stapled it to the posts. Finally, they ran two strands of barbed wire round the field above the netting, one strand on the outside of the posts and the other on the inside. Ambrose had never done any fencing work before but he was quick to catch on. He had an instinct for knowing what needed to be done and then doing it. For a long time they worked in silence.

'I was pleased you had work for me today,' Ambrose said finally.

'Why is that?'

'Well, I need the money. I haven't had many offers of work since my arrest.'

'Money is scarce,' Tom said. 'We could all do with some more of it.'

'It isn't just that. People think I'm the murderer. I can see it in their faces.'

'I'll be pleased when the guards arrest whoever did it. As it is, we're all under suspicion, all in the same boat.'

'Surely no one suspects you,' Ambrose said.

'I don't know.'

'Do you think I'm guilty?'

'No man is guilty till he's convicted.'

'It isn't that simple,' Ambrose said. 'In a place like this where everyone knows everyone else, the stranger will always be the first suspect.'

Tom felt uneasy about the conversation. He found himself saying things that he did not wish to say.

'I think you're wasting your time here, a fine young fellow like you. You have too much time on your hands. Too much brooding never did any man any good.'

'I came here to write, and that's what I'm doing.'

'A man needs work that pays, work that puts something in the pot. What did you do before you came here?'

'I worked in advertising.'

'And what did you have to do all day?'

'Think up slogans for advertisements.'

'Like "O'Donnell Abu!" and "Up Dev!"?'

'No, slogans like "Guinness is good for you."'

'You must be a journalist, then. My son's a journalist. You know Jim, don't you?'

'He's a real journalist, a newspaper journalist. I was trying to make people buy things they didn't need. I felt I was getting paid to tell lies. That's why I packed it in.'

'You should talk to Jim next time he's home. I'm sure he could give you good advice. There must be lots of jobs you could do in Dublin.'

He didn't know why he said it. Maybe it was just because he felt for the lad. Ambrose wasn't a bad sort. He was obviously worried, and not without reason. Looking at him and talking to him, Tom couldn't help feeling that he was like everyone else, doing his best to keep his head above water. He was calm and level-headed, and likeable in his way.

That night Tom lay awake for a long time. He kept thinking about Ambrose and the kind of man he was. In the morning he told himself that thinking was getting him nowhere. There were puzzles in every man's life that no amount of thinking would solve.

It wasn't a good day for writing. He had been at it since early morning and all he had to show for his labour was one short paragraph. He ate a slice of bread and drank a mug of water. He told Sharon that he was going for a walk on the hill.

He headed north, keeping to the jagged coastline. He tried not to think about his writing, and instead forced himself to take note of the rock shapes below, the hurrying clouds above, and the changing conformation of the land. After an hour he turned inland and found himself on a height, looking down on a little glen with a stream running through it to the sea. It was a grey day. Visibility wasn't all that good, and he had to look twice to make sure that what he really saw rising before him was smoke. It seemed to be coming from behind a rock about five hundred yards away. It was grey like the day, but still noticeable against the reddish-brown of the landscape. It was rising, not in a straggly line, but in little puffs as if from the pipe of a furious smoker. Somewhat mystified, he stood looking at it for a good five minutes. Then he began walking slowly down the slope.

As he drew closer, he could see that it was rising out of what looked like a hole in the ground. Suddenly, it dawned on him that it must be what the locals called a still-house. It was facing north, a bothie between two rocks with a flat roof of heathery scraws and a makeshift hole for a chimney. He stood in the doorway and peered into the smoky gloom beyond.

'What takes you out here now?' Muiris emerged from semi-darkness.

'I was out walking and saw the smoke.'

'You know what they say about the cat? Curiosity killed her.' Muiris was standing at the opening, smiling ambiguously His nose looked sharper than usual, and the hollows below his cheekbones darker.

'My aunt always said it was care that killed the cat.'

'She was wrong there. It was curiosity. If you take good care of a cat, she'll outlive you.'

'But too much worry will kill anyone,' Ambrose said.

'I never worry. Do you know why? As a young man I never had any reason to.'

He could see that Muiris wasn't going to invite him in. He looked round, wondering what to say next.

'You must be thirsty after your walk,' Muiris said. 'I suppose you could be doing with a drink?'

'To tell the truth, I wouldn't mind a drink.'

Muiris vanished into the gloom and came out with a ten-glass bottle containing a clear liquor like water. Ambrose extracted the cork and raised the bottle to his nose.

'It isn't perfume. It's meant to be drunk.'

Ambrose took a slug, which scorched his throat and ignited a ball of fire in the pit of his stomach.

'It's good,' he managed to gasp.

'You'll get nothing but the best from me.'

'Do you make it from barley?'

'No.'

'You must make it from potatoes, then?'

'No.'

'What do you make it from?'

'That's my secret. Every distiller has his own recipe. There's more than one way to skin a cat.'

'It's a good cat, however it was skinned.' Ambrose put the cork back in the bottle.

'You'll be going another bit now,' Muiris said. 'But as Christ said to the disciples, tell no man what you've seen or heard.'

He hurried up the slope and did not turn round till he had reached the top. There he stood, looking down on the rising smoke, not quite knowing what to think. Then it occurred to him that perhaps Muiris had given him the germ of a story.

Cormac Gildea and Marcus Quinn were stretched in the lea of a rock, smoking their pipes, looking down on the shore where a lone figure was walking along the drift-line with his head bent.

'What's he up to?' Marcus wondered.

'Maybe he's waiting for cast-in,' Cormac smiled.

'He'll be waiting a long time, and the wind from the east.'

'He's probably collecting driftwood for the fire. You'd think it would be less trouble to steal a creel of turf from a neighbour.'

They both looked at each other and laughed.

'Strange how little a man knows about what goes on behind his back,' Marcus said.

'It depends on the man,' Cormac assured him. 'Some men don't give any cause.'

'Would you say he's guilty?' Marcus asked.

'What do you think?'

'I'm not sure. To listen to him you'd think butter wouldn't melt in his mouth.'

'Well, I'm sure,' Cormac said. 'Who else would do it but a foreigner? It's Agent Cox all over again.'

'You'll be voting for the Triangle, so?'

'Won't you?'

'It's a big decision.'

Cormac looked at his friend. They always saw eye to eye, and they always helped each other with work that two men could do more efficiently than one. Marcus lent his long ladder to Cormac whenever his house needed thatching, and Cormac let Marcus have the grazing of Páirc a' Tobair for his cow for nothing.

'Would you believe it? Neil Durkin was enquiring about the grazing of Páirc a' Tobair,' Cormac said suddenly.

'What did he want?'

'He wanted to know how much it would cost for a year.'

'What did you say?'

'I told him you had first refusal.' Cormac looked at his friend who was still looking down on the solitary figure on the shore.

'How much will you be wanting for it?' Marcus asked slowly.

'You can have it again this year for nothing. We must all stick together,' Cormac said.

'I suppose we must,' said Marcus.

Muiris wasn't happy. He had found two lambs dead on the hill with their eyes picked out by the crows. They had been weak at birth, and he knew he should have taken them down to the house. He had thought about it but he'd felt tired at the time and there were other things on his mind. As a rule he was not a man much given to self-accusation, but he had high expectations, and mistakes that could have been avoided always gnawed at his gizzard. He turned and saw Neil Durkin coming towards him up the slope.

'Bloody crows,' he said. 'You can't turn your back for a minute.'

'They're worse than the fox,' Neil Durkin was short and squat. He looked up at Muiris for a split second, then concentrated his gaze on the top button of his waistcoat.

'Did you lose any?'

'Four so far. Look at that ewe of mine over there. This is her third year without carrying. I wouldn't mind only she takes the ram every time, the game little devil.'

'Ewes are like women. Some are natural mothers, some aren't.' Muiris spoke with an upward tilt of the chin, as if he had uttered a truth not known to lesser men.

'She'll make mutton broth one of these days. It's all she's good for. Maybe you'd do the butchering, if you have the time.'

'She isn't ripe for butchering,' Muiris said. 'Leave her for a month or two till she puts on a bit of weight after the long winter.'

'We'll leave her till the end of June, then.'

'Have you come to any conclusions, Neil?'

'Conclusions?'

'About Ambrose.'

'Ah, you mean the Triangle? I've been busy, I haven't had time to think.'

'Neighbours like us must stand shoulder to shoulder, Neil. You know I'll always give you a hand. Any time you want help, it's yours for the asking. I can't say better than that.'

'You'll do the butchering then?'

'I will and welcome, Neil.'

'And you can have any cut you like. You can have a leg, if that's what takes your fancy.'

'And you'll think about the Triangle.'

'I will.'

'Good man yourself. A good neighbour is worth more than a mountain of sheep.'

Nick had been fishing for over an hour from the Leic Chrochta, a broad, flat rock about ten feet above water at high tide. An overhanging platform at the end of an exposed headland, it cantilevered out to such an extent that when you peered over the edge you could not see its base. It was an ideal rock for fishing; it could easily accommodate four men standing side by side with hand-lines. Today he had it all to himself, facing the blank Atlantic while to right and left rose the indomitable grey cliffs with their crazily inclined folds, as if Nature herself were an eccentric brickie, laying down strata one by one with a trowel. He loved being on his own here, alone with sea and sky, at one with nature and the world, at one with the whole human race. Here petty quarrels and thoughts of personal defeat evaporated in the keenly cutting air, while every discordant note from the past drowned in the overwhelming music of the sea. He could spend his whole life here, if only life could always be like this. He had never felt such deep, deep peace anywhere, but the snatched half-hour of bliss was not the whole inexorable story.

Patrick McGinley

Tom Barron had told him that the hand-line was best for the Leic Chrochta but he had brought a byan rod as well to be on the safe side. The byan rod was stiff, unlike a bamboo rod, because a whippy rod would be no good for byan, which was the local name for a species of wrasse. Tom had said that he had caught byan from the Leic Chrochta in August but he doubted if they would be plentiful at this time of year. Today he had caught a medium-sized pollock with the second shot of the hand-line, but after an hour's fruitless effort he examined his lure again, wondering if perhaps it stank. Then it occurred to him that he might have caught the only fish this side of the Tor Mór. It was a depressing thought and he told himself it could not conceivably be true. The pollock would be enough for Sharon and Emily's dinner but he needed something for himself as well.

His trousers were wet from the hand-line, which wouldn't matter so much if he had a worthwhile catch to take home. He wound the hand-line round its frame and put it aside. Reaching down into his sack, he took out one of the two of the partans he had caught in a rock pool that morning while the tide was out. He banged the partan with a stone to break its shell and tied a chunk of its flesh to the byan hook with a length of thread. The water around the Leic Chrochta was deep. He dropped the sink in the water and waited as it took the baited hook to the bottom where the byan were supposed to feed. Raising the rod about eighteen inches or so, as Tom Barron had taught him, so that the bait was left dangling just above the bottom, he held the rod firmly with both hands, lifting and lowering it ever so slowly. He felt like saying a little prayer, but he knew it wouldn't work because normally he didn't believe in prayer. Instead he said to himself, 'I hope the byan are as hungry as I am.'

Gradually, he forgot about his hunger. His mind emptied as the rhythm of the fishing took over. After a while he thought he felt a little nibble but it could just have been the current tugging at the line. He held the rod steady for a moment, then raised it with a little jerk. His wrist came alive as the line went taut. He caught the line in one hand, dropped the rod behind him, and hauled in the line hand over hand. It was a fine strong byan with thick lips and coarse reddish scales like chain-mail. He unhooked it carefully so as to avoid the spines before putting it in the bag with the pollock. Neither Sharon nor Emily would eat byan because of its strong flavour, so he would have it all to himself. He would be home by half-past four, in good time to gut both fish and prepare them for Sharon's version of fish cookery.

He sat down on the rock and listened to the fluttering of the gasping fish in the bag. Now he knew why Tom Barron always lit his pipe after laying down his rod. He himself was not a smoker but he felt that somehow the ritual in which he had participated remained incomplete, that he should do something else to bring a perfect afternoon to its destined conclusion. It was strange how the byan had come to him while his mind was blank. He had been fishing mechanically, going through the motions with his eye on the empty horizon. Then suddenly, a strike! That's how stories came to him, always while he was thinking of something else. Just as the byan came up to him out of the depth of darkness, a story often overtook him unexpectedly on the road, stealing up behind him and pouncing while his mind was on other things. That was life at its best, life as it should be lived every day.

Sharon was washing her hair when he got home, and Emily was colouring a picture in the little book he'd bought her. He gutted the fish and washed them in cold water flavoured with a pinch of coarse salt. Then he cut off the heads because Sharon didn't like looking at what she called 'the sorrowful eyes'. That done, he settled down to write a short story about an inexperienced tourist who'd lost his way in the hills in a fog, and as if by magic came upon a still-house and a mysterious poteen-maker who promptly sent him on his way with complicated directions and a consolatory bottle. When the tourist arrived back at his hotel, he told his fellow guests about his adventure. He offered them a drink from the bottle and discovered that the liquor it contained was nothing less than pure spring water. They laughed at his surprise and told him he'd imagined it all.

Over dinner he said to Sharon that it was time they sent Emily to school. She was lively and bright, and she would benefit from the company of other children.

'She'd learn nothing of any use at school,' Sharon said. 'Everything is taught here through the medium of Irish. What good is that to her, I'd like to know?'

'I'm learning Irish myself,' he said. 'I could help her learn while I'm teaching myself.'

'You're quite cuckoo, Nick. I for one have no intention of enduring another winter here.'

'Give yourself time. As you get to know more people, you'll settle in.'

'Unlike you, I have no intention of going native. There's nothing here except hills and sheep and old men. This isn't living. We're only existing from one day to the next… '

It was always the same with Sharon. No matter what subject he brought up, she would bring the conversation round to the misery of life in Leaca. It was such a shame because there was no other girl remotely like her.

10

Muiris was in his armchair holding forth with all the authority of a bishop on his episcopal throne. He had a lean face with a clean jaw line, and whenever he clenched his teeth, which he did with predictable regularity, you could see his maxillary muscles ripple beneath the tight skin. Having poured poteen for his neighbours with his customary generosity, he himself partook judiciously of a hot whiskey with cloves and sugar.

'I must tell you a good one before I forget,' he said. 'Here was I making a wee run out in sight of Loch an Aifrinn, thinking I had the mountain to myself, when who darkens the still-house door but my bold Ambrose.'

'Ah, go 'way!' Cormac exclaimed.

'Not a word of a lie. And he'd have come in to see what was going on if I hadn't blocked the doorway. "Curiosity killed the cat", says I.'

'I'll bet he had no answer to that,' Neil Durkin smiled.

'He had an answer all right. Bold as brass, he told me it was care that killed him.'

'Sure that makes no sense at all.'

'I told him that if you take good care of a cat, he'll live longer than yourself, because a cat has nine lives as every galoot should know.'

'You were fit for him, Muiris, fair play to you.'

'I wanted to get rid of him without letting him see what I was doing, so I gave him a bottle of the bucko and sent him on his way.'

'I hope you gave him the singlings!' Marcus laughed.

'Or the dirty drop!' Cormac suggested.

'I gave him the best, the very best, because it isn't in my nature to give any man less, and anyway I didn't want him going round saying my poteen is horse piss. And do you know what I'm going to tell you? He took one slug and nearly choked on it!' Muiris slapped his thigh and showed his teeth in silent laughter. It was a laugh peculiar to himself, which involved a wrinkling of the nostrils, a swelling of the stomach, and a nervous trembling of the lower jaw. Everyone who knew Muiris knew when he was laughing, though no sound would emerge from between his lips. A laugh from Muiris was a signal for other men to laugh in appreciation, which his neighbours duly did, but whether they were laughing at what made Muiris laugh or at his way of laughing was anyone's guess.

'And what took him out to Loch an Aifrinn?' Marcus wondered.

'No one knows what that man is thinking,' Muiris said. 'He's foxier than any fox. He could even have been looking for Agent Cox's grave. Some men can foresee things before they have time to happen.'

'He was up to nothing good, whatever it was,' Cormac said. 'Wasn't he down on the strand a couple of days ago pretending to be looking for cast-in and the wind from the east!'

'Maybe he was looking for driftwood for the fire,' Daniel said. 'There's nothing wrong with that, is there?'

'It's better than stealing a creel of your turf, if that's what you mean,' Cormac agreed.

'Ambrose was working for you the other day, Tom. Did you notice anything strange about him?' Muiris asked.

'He's a worried man,' Tom said. 'He's trying to make a living with the pen and not making much fist of it. He has to rely on the rest of us for the odd day's pay.'

'Sure, everyone knows that the spade is mightier than the pen. So what did you talk about?' Muiris asked.

'He told me he used to work in advertising. He got paid to think up a new slogan every day. He thought up "Guinness is good for you."'

'I must get him to think up a slogan for my poteen,' Muiris smiled. 'The man's a lunatic. Didn't he come down the road the other day talking his head off and not another soul in sight.'

'He makes up stories and writes them down,' Tom said. 'In his way he's a kind of shanachie, I suppose.'

'Shanachie, my foot! There's no need to make up more stories,' Cormac said. 'The old stories are good enough for any man.'

'I wouldn't agree there,' Tom said. 'Aren't the newspapers full of new stories every day?'

'I think you're becoming too fond of Ambrose,' Muiris advised. 'He's cleverer than you think. If you're not careful, he'll soon have you in his pocket.'

'There's no danger of that,' Tom said. 'I listen to what every man has to say and then make up my own mind.'

Muiris gave him a long look of dry appraisal.

'It's over a month since Paddy Canty was murdered and there's still no sign of the murderer being arrested,' he said. 'The police have made a hames of the investigation. First, they arrested Red Miller instead of Ambrose. When they finally arrested Ambrose, they let him go again. Now, believe it or not, they're looking for a man on a motorbike! Sure, they're only going through the motions, they don't know what they're doing. It's up to us to get justice for Paddy. We all know who did it, it's as clear as day. There's no point waiting any longer. Like our grandfathers before us, we must carry out the sentence ourselves.'

'What does that mean?' Daniel asked.

'The Triangle, that's what it means.' For a moment there was total silence as Muiris surveyed the faces before him.

'You realise what you're saying?' Daniel said. 'If we go for the Triangle, we'll all be guilty of murder before the fact.'

'What fact would that be now?' Cormac wondered.

'We'll be guilty of conspiracy to murder,' Daniel explained.

'We'll be putting right a terrible wrong, according to the ancient law of the land. We'll all take an envelope from the pile and the man who gets the Triangle in the Circle will carry out the sentence. And the beauty of it is that none of us will know which of us it is.' Muiris thrust out his chin and turned to Daniel.

'It's still murder in my book,' Daniel said.

'Your book is written in English, then,' Muiris told him. 'There's only one law in Leaca and it's written in Irish. It's called *dlí na féine*, Brehon law.'

'There was no capital punishment under Brehon law,' the schoolmaster said.

'I know the Brehon law,' Muiris insisted. 'It was handed down in my family. My people were Brehons before me.'

'Brehon or no Brehon, it's still murder,' Daniel said. 'It will follow you like a shadow for as long as you live. You'll never be able to forget it. On your deathbed it will stare you in the face.'

'Did the man who executed Agent Cox have it on his conscience?' Muiris asked.

'Maybe he did. We don't know.'

'Agent Cox was different,' Tom Barron said. 'The country was under foreign rule then and the foreigner wasn't welcome. Ambrose is harmless. Like the rest of us, he's only doing his best to make ends meet.'

'Does that mean stealing other people's turf and breaking into their houses in the small hours with nothing but robbery and murder on your mind?'

'Where's the proof?' Daniel demanded. 'If there was any proof against him, he'd have been arrested long ago.'

'Who's doing it then, if it isn't Ambrose? Do you think it's me?'

'I wouldn't accuse you without proof positive,' Daniel said.

'You should have been a lawyer,' Muiris scoffed. 'Isn't that what's wrong with English law? When the lawyers get going, certainty flies out the window. They'll always find a hundred excuses for reasonable doubt.'

'I'd rather live with reasonable doubt than a miscarriage of justice. In my view justice should be left to judges and juries.'

'If that's what you think, you should go home to your books,' Muiris said.

'Books have nothing to do with it but right thinking has.' Daniel put down his glass and said good night.

When he had gone, Muiris declared that anyone who agreed with the schoolmaster should leave the meeting. When no one moved, he gave Tom Barron one of his searching looks.

'Are you staying, Tom?' he asked.

'I'll stay,' Tom said, though he was far from sure why he'd said it. He felt uneasy over the turn the conversation had taken. There was no talking to Muiris in one of his Brehon moods.

Muiris asked each of them in turn if he was ready for the Triangle, and each of them said yes. Then he poured more poteen and told them he was going to get the envelopes from the bedroom. While he was gone, they talked in low voices and looked into the fire rather than at one another. They all looked serious. For want of something better to do, Neil Durkin took an armful of turf from the galley rod basket in the corner and replenished the fire. After a while Muiris returned with five envelopes, which he put in an empty bucket that stood on the form by the back door.

'There's a sheet of notepaper in every envelope,' he said. 'I've drawn a circle the size of a half-crown on every sheet and a triangle inside the circle on only one of them. Every man will take an envelope from the bucket as he leaves. The one that's left will be mine. No man must tell any other man what was in his envelope. Whoever gets the triangle must carry out the sentence alone.'

'What is the sentence?' Neil Durkin asked uncertainly.

'According to Brehon law, a murderer must get the same treatment he gave his victim. Paddy was strangled. Is that clear?'

'I think it is,' Neil Durkin said.

'It couldn't be clearer,' Cormac said. 'Death by strangling.'

Sharing a sense of having opened a new chapter in local history, they drank their poteen and talked about other things. They all looked serious, as if they could think of nothing but the envelopes in the bucket. Towards midnight they said good night to Muiris and headed home.

Tom could think only of the terrible decision they had come to and the slim envelope in his inside pocket. It was as if he had woken up from a nightmare that now did not seem possible. His stiff leg was giving him trouble again and he was sweating, though the night was cold. When he reached the yard, he hesitated before going into the house. Instead he went into the barn and opened the envelope. He struck a match and held up the flame before the single sheet. He had drawn the one with the triangle. The real nightmare, the living, waking nightmare, had begun.

11

'Can't you sleep?' Nancy said. 'You're keeping everyone awake, shaking the bed and puffing and rolling like a whale.'

'It's my leg again,' he said.

'Or too much poteen! You never sleep well after raking with Muiris. Turn on your side and think of Jim when he was a boy. That's what I always do.'

He hated secrecy and the need to keep her in the dark. She had asked him who was at Muiris Mór's, and he had told her there were only the two of them. If he had said there was a meeting, she would have given him no peace, wanting to know what was discussed and who said this and who said that. He did his best to think of Jim as a boy but he could only think of Ambrose and Muiris, two impossible men. It was all very well making big talk about the Triangle and the time of Agent Cox, but you couldn't kill a man in cold blood. It wasn't right; it was against all instinct and sense of what should be done and what shouldn't. He blamed himself for having stayed on at the meeting. He should have left with the schoolmaster when he'd had a chance. He pulled the bed-spread up over his head, hoping against hope that he would sleep.

He spent the following day on the hill with the dog as his only companion. By evening he had come to a decision. He would ask Ambrose to give him a hand thatching the old house, which he now used as a barn. He would talk to Ambrose and listen to him and keep a clear head. He would not be swayed by Muiris and the others. He would make up his own mind. It stood to reason that a guilty man couldn't hide his guilt.

Ambrose arrived while they were having breakfast. Nancy gave him a mug of tea, and when she offered him a thick slice of buttered soda bread to go with it, he didn't say no. Quite possibly, the poor devil had had no breakfast at home.

'Not a bad day,' he remarked as he tucked in.

'It's dry and calm, and that's what counts,' Tom said. 'The last thing you need for thatching is wind.'

When they'd eaten, Tom took him out to the barn to show him the side that needed thatching. Ambrose remarked that it was a fine old house, and Tom told him that it was once the family home and that the new house had been built by his father when he himself was a boy. He gave him Jim's scythe because he was about the same height as Jim. Ambrose tried out the scythe in the yard, and Tom told him it was just right, that it could have been hung specially for him. He had taught Ambrose how to mow with a scythe last summer. At first he looked awkward, holding the scythe with the tip of the blade pointing downwards. Tom showed him how to keep the heel of the scythe as close as possible to the ground with the tip of the blade slightly raised. To give him his due, he didn't need telling twice. After half an hour's practice he was a capable scytheman, though his gait of mowing was still a bit stiff with the result that he probably expended more energy than was strictly necessary. He had strength to burn, however. If he didn't, he wouldn't be burning it.

Tom took him down to the sand dunes at the bottom of the farm, which had been taken over by bent-grass. There they set to work. He showed Ambrose the type of bent that was best for thatching and instructed him to cut only the best. It was not the best time of year for cutting bent. It was a job he should have done the previous autumn but he had been busy with other things at the time. In early February a night of 'big wind' had ruffled the thatch of the barn. In the calm of the following day he had done his best to repair the damage here and there, but now he felt it was time to make it more secure.

Ambrose concentrated on the cutting, while Tom followed behind, gathering the best of the bent and tying it in bunches with lengths of rope. They worked steadily for two hours without saying much. When he had gathered enough of the bent, they carried the bound bunches up to the yard. It was after midday when they made the last trip, and not long afterwards Nancy called them in for a dinner of salt cod, potatoes and turnip.

Ambrose said that he loved salt cod, that he'd had it in Portugal once. The Portuguese, he said, were so fond of it that they ate it at Christmas and called it their 'faithful friend'.

'You mean to say they prefer it to chicken or goose?' Nancy said.

'They take their salt cod seriously. They even have different grades of it in the shops.'

'It's a nuisance to cook,' Nancy said. 'You have to soak it in water overnight and change the water two or three times. I like fresh cod, though, but I prefer chicken. There's nothing better than a young chicken. I could eat chicken every day of the year if I could get it.'

'My favourite fish is byan,' Ambrose said. 'I caught a whopper from the Leic Chrochta the other day. It made two good meals for me because Sharon and Emily don't eat it.'

'You've become a real Leaca man,' Nancy said. 'Eating byan and big fish for your dinner.'

'I'd eat sand-eels if I could get them. I had them down below in the glen once. They looked like little eels on my plate and they tasted of turf smoke. The man who gave them to me said they're very good raw with poteen.'

'Surely, you don't drink poteen,' Nancy smiled.

'Only when I can get it. Muiris gave me a bottle the other day. At first I thought it was water because he didn't say it was poteen. He handed it to me as if he were giving me a drink from a spring well. He's a very generous man is Muiris.'

'Mind yourself on Muiris. He's generous only when it suits him,' Nancy said. 'If you know what's good for you, you'll stay well clear of his poteen. It's ruined more families than I could name in a week.'

As he listened to Nancy, Tom realised, and not for the first time, that he was married to a very special woman. She was talking to Ambrose as if he were her son. Nancy was like no other woman he knew. No wonder Muiris never looked twice at any other girl after losing her. There were certain men for whom there was only one woman. Like Muiris, he himself was one of them. He reckoned he was a very lucky man.

When they had cleared their plates, Nancy gave them tea and a good slice of the barmbrack she had baked the previous evening. He could see that Ambrose liked talking to her. His eye followed her as she went about the kitchen, clearing up after they'd eaten. Tom couldn't help thinking that he was the kind of man who was totally devoid of malice. He couldn't imagine him doing any man a bad turn let alone serious injury. He couldn't believe that this was the man they had all been plotting against the previous evening. He felt deeply ashamed, not just of himself but of Muiris and his neighbours.

They didn't linger in the kitchen. Tom got out the ladder and they took the ropes off the thatch on the south side of the barn. He began thatching while Ambrose tended, bringing up one bunch of bent-grass at a time and moving the ladder as required. Ambrose told him that where he came from, bent-grass was called marram. After that they didn't talk much; each remained absorbed in his task. Clouds had piled in from the sea. Though they didn't look like rain clouds, Tom was taking no chances. He worked quickly and efficiently, and Ambrose was there with another bunch whenever he was ready for it. When he had finished, they put fresh straw ropes over the thatch and tied them to the stone pins that jutted from the walls. Tom stood and looked at his handiwork, saying that it was a job better done than left for tomorrow.

'It was well judged,' Ambrose smiled. 'There are only two bunches left over.'

'They won't go to waste. They'll do for patching.'

It was already dark when they sat down to tea. Tom felt better now. He had come to a decision that cleared his mind of the dark thoughts that had been weighing him down.

'Will you write about today when you go home?' he asked Ambrose.

'I won't write about it yet. I'll allow the dust to settle first. I'll be able to see it more clearly then. At the moment I'm writing about the Sunday afternoon last September when everyone piled into Daniel's kitchen to listen to the All-Ireland Football Final.'

'It was a good match,' Tom said. 'Played in the Polo Grounds, New York, no less. I thought Muiris would have a fit when Kerry lost.'

'Why did he support Kerry when everyone else was rooting for Cavan?'

'Muiris likes to be different,' Nancy said. 'He thinks it's a sign of strength.'

'I'll never forget the tension,' Ambrose said. 'Everyone was on tenterhooks, including Michael O'Hehir. It was the best commentary I ever heard. He had to beg for more time at the end.'

'And he got it, too. There would have been civil war if he hadn't.'

Tom and Ambrose spent half an hour discussing the match while Nancy listened. It seemed to Tom that Ambrose remembered every kick and pass. For a man who wasn't brought up playing Gaelic football, he had an extraordinary knowledge of the game. Tom found himself warming to him. He might be a bit odd in his ways, walking the hills on his own at all hours, but at heart he was like Jim or any other young man.

The following day he met Muiris on the hill, while they were both out counting their lambs.

'If it isn't the crows, it's the fox,' Muiris said. 'I lost a fine ram lamb yesterday. Taken while my back was turned.'

'That lamb of mine looks weak. I must move herself and her mother down to the park,' Tom said. He wanted to talk to Muiris but he did not know how to begin.

'Ambrose is still around, I see. Whoever got the Triangle is taking his time.'

'That's what I wanted to tell you, Muiris. I can't do it.'

'So it was you who got it? I knew you were too close to him. The hangman doesn't invite the murderer to dinner before the morning of the day.'

'It isn't that. I don't think he did it. It would be killing an innocent man.'

'Innocent, my arse. You were always a softie, Tom.'

'I had a long conversation with Ambrose yesterday. He may be a bit strange in his ways but he wouldn't hurt a fly. He doesn't think like the rest of us. When you see him out walking on his own, all he's doing is thinking up stories to write down.'

'Well, he made up a story that's convinced you all right.' Muiris bared his teeth in silent laughter.

'The Triangle was fine under the old landlords when the law was made by Englishmen for their own protection. Now the law is for everyone. We live in a different world, Muiris.'

'It's still English law. It was taken over lock, stock and barrel by the Dáil. In Leaca there's only one law while I'm still around. The old Brehon law. I'll call another meeting. You needn't worry, I won't ask you to come.'

Muiris struck his boot with the ferrule of his crook. His dog took it as a signal to get up and follow him. Tom stood watching as man and dog zigzagged down the hillside along the narrow track. In spite of everything, he felt better for having spoken to Muiris. It was a load off his mind, but only until he asked himself: what would happen to Ambrose now?

12

Muiris began by pouring the usual drinks. He reached for the poteen bottle, which he kept behind the curtain of the kitchen bed, and filled three glasses. He poured himself a small whiskey and topped it up with hot water from the kettle, as was his wont.

'No cloves tonight?' Cormac remarked.

'I'm out of cloves and sugar. I must go to the shop tomorrow for some more. Whiskey without cloves isn't whiskey.'

'Have you ever put them in poteen?' Neil Durkin asked with a sly glance at his host.

'There's no need,' Muiris assured him. 'My poteen is perfection as it is.' He looked serious and preoccupied. For a while he listened to the conversation of the others without saying much.

'Isn't Tom coming?' Cormac asked.

'Tom drew the Triangle at the last meeting,' Muiris said. 'He came to me yesterday saying he wouldn't be carrying out the sentence.'

'Did he say why?' Cormac asked.

'We all know Tom. He got too close to Ambrose. He sees him as another son.'

'Jim had better look out.' Cormac laughed and so did Marcus.

'Did he say he wouldn't or couldn't carry out the sentence?' Neil Durkin asked.

'What does that mean?' Muiris demanded.

'Well, maybe he thinks Ambrose is innocent. He knows him better than any of us.'

'Do you think he's innocent?' Muiris enquired.

'I'm not sure,' Neil Durkin said. 'No one can be absolutely sure.'

'Well, I'm sure. I suppose you think I did it? Or was it Cormac or Marcus there? Or maybe it was Daniel Burke or Tom Barron himself!'

'It could be someone from below in the glen,' Neil said.

'Or it could be a man on a motorbike! It could even be Sergeant McNally!' Muiris scoffed.

Cormac slapped his palm against his thigh and laughed.

'We began with six. Now there's only four of us left,' Neil Durkin said.

'What difference does that make?' Muiris shifted his weight from his right buttock to his left and reached for his pipe.

'Tom must have had good reason for refusing to do it. He's honest, is Tom. I'd be inclined to respect his opinion.'

'Maybe he was afeard,' Muiris said. 'Tom was never one to run a risk.'

'I think Neil has a point,' Cormac said. 'Now that we're just four, the odds on drawing the Triangle are shorter.'

'I want every man to ask himself two questions,' Muiris summed up. 'Did Ambrose do it? And am I willing to stand up like a man to get justice for Paddy Canty?' If you can't answer yes to both questions, I'd like to know.'

He topped up their glasses from the poteen bottle. He still hadn't touched his whiskey. Then he asked both questions of each of them in turn, beginning with Cormac. They all said they believed Ambrose was the murderer, but when it came to the question of doing something about it, none of them was willing to stick his neck out.

'Now at least we know where we stand,' Muiris said.

'Would you do it, if you got the Triangle?' Neil Durkin asked.

'As I see it, what needs to be done must be done. I'd carry out the sentence as our forefathers did, and I think I know another man who'd do the same.'

'Who?' Cormac asked.

'Red Miller, who else?'

'Be the hokey, you could be right.'

'Miller was no friend of Paddy Canty's,' Neil Durkin reminded them.

'Beggars can't be choosers. We'll have another meeting tomorrow evening and I'll invite him. Then at least we'll have five instead of four.'

'It won't make any difference unless he gets the Triangle, and there's only one chance in five of that happening,' Neil Durkin said.

'He'll get it all right,' Muiris told him. 'I'll make sure he does.'

For a moment there was silence while everyone pondered how this most desirable of impossibilities might be achieved.

'I don't understand how you can be so sure,' Cormac said.

'It's very simple,' Muiris explained. 'Everyone will get a Triangle but only Red Miller will act on it.'

'It's a terrible trick to play on any man,' Neil Durkin said with genuine concern.

'No, it isn't. Like Tom Barron before him, he'll be free to carry out the sentence or not as the case may be. No one is holding a gun to his head. It's entirely up to him.'

'I see what you mean,' Cormac said. 'We're appointing Miller as executioner but we're leaving the choice to him.'

'He'll think the rest of us got Circles without a Triangle,' Neil Durkin said. 'Is that fair?'

'No man ever lost sleep over something he didn't know,' Muiris said. 'Who's to tell him unless you do?'

'You're right,' Cormac said. 'If he avenges Paddy's death, he'll only be making up for all the trouble he made over fences while Paddy was alive.'

'That's how I see it as well,' Muiris said. 'We're doing Miller a favour. And we're killing two birds with one stone.'

A dog barked twice, and Muiris raised his hand for silence. The dog barked again.

'That's Bran's bark,' Muiris said. 'I'll go out to see what's wrong.'

He took his shotgun from behind the curtain and released the safety-catch. Then he opened the door and vanished into the night. The other men looked at one another. Cormac smiled and Marcus laughed uncertainly.

'I think he means business,' Neil Durkin said.

'If he means business, he's going a bit far,' Cormac reasoned.

'Maybe he's just trying to impress us,' Marcus smiled.

'The question is: are we all going a bit far with the Triangle?' Neil Durkin put on a serious face. 'It isn't fair on Red Miller. It's a foul trick to play on him.'

'We're not putting any pressure on him. We're just giving him an opportunity to show his true colours,' Cormac said.

'Would you murder a man in cold blood?' Neil Durkin asked.

'It depends.'

'Depends on what?'

'If he murdered my brother or a member of my family, I'd top and tail him just like a turnip,' Cormac said. 'What about you? Would you execute a murderer who was beyond the reach of the law?'

'No, I couldn't do it,' Neil Durkin said. 'We should remember that there's no hangman in Ireland. Pierpoint comes over from England to do the job. Hanging is a dirty business. It's murder no matter how you look at it.'

The door opened again and Muiris entered with his gun on his arm.

'It was Bran all right. It must have been the fox that disturbed him. Lucky for him there's no moon. If there was, he'd have got both barrels up the arse.'

Muiris put the shotgun back behind the curtain and returned to his chair in the corner. He raised his glass and held it up against the light, savouring the taste in advance of putting it to his thin lips.

'We all need to be on our guard,' he said. 'With a murderer on the loose, we can't afford to dally. We'll meet at nine again tomorrow evening.'

Red Miller was first to arrive. Muiris put him sitting in the armchair on the side of the fire opposite his own. He was a bulky man who seemed to be on the point of bursting through his tight-fitting clothes. He had a big, round face with red, curly hair and he rested a big freckled hand on each of his knees. Muiris told him that he'd laid down poison for the fox, and Miller said he himself had done the same.

'Madge had a chicken that died with the disorder,' he smiled. 'I looked at her and said she'll make a fine dinner for the fox.'

The others trooped in one by one. When Muiris had got everyone a drink, he explained the purpose of the meeting with his customary air of magisterial authority. Red Miller asked if Tom Barron and Daniel Burke would be coming, and Muiris told him that they were both friendly with Ambrose and had begged to be excused.

'Like Tom, I get Ambrose to do a day's work for me now and again but I always keep my distance. Give every man his due and no man more. That's my policy,' Muiris added.

'It's a good policy,' Cormac agreed. 'It keeps everything simple, and that's how everything should be.'

There was a lengthy debate as to whether Ambrose was guilty, to which everyone contributed his mite of wisdom. Then came the vexed question of what to do about it, since the guards didn't seem to be doing anything. Only after many shades of opinion had been aired and scrutinised did Muiris introduce the question of the Triangle.

'It's a risky business,' Red Miller said.

'It's as safe as houses,' Muiris assured him. 'No one will know who drew the Triangle except the man who drew it. Before we say good night, we'll all swear on the book never to tell anyone else what we drew.'

'Someone is bound to find out,' Miller said.

'Did anyone ever find out who killed Agent Cox?' Muiris asked. 'The peelers certainly didn't, and they combed every inch of the countryside. I had that from my own grandfather when he was ninety and sitting in the chair you're sitting in now.'

'But if anything happens to Ambrose, we'll all be questioned again,' Miller reasoned. 'Two murders in quick succession. There will be stories in the papers and all hell breaking loose.'

'It's easy enough hoodwinking the guards. If there's no body, there can be no murder.'

'You mean they'll think he's vanished?' Miller said.

'They'll think he skedaddled back to England. It will prove to them beyond doubt that he murdered Paddy Canty and was afraid to face the music of the law.'

'It's still risky,' Red Miller said. 'Hiding a body isn't easy. Someone would be bound to come across it.'

'We're blest with miles and miles of bog and mountain,' Muiris said. 'If I get the Triangle, I've already got a quiet little spot in mind that no one knows about except myself.'

'Loch an Aifrinn would make a fine resting place,' Neil Durkin pointed out. 'You could weigh the body down with stones, and it's got a lovely soft bottom for the stones to sink in.'

'We won't mention places,' Muiris said. 'Let every man settle on his own favourite spot and keep it to himself. That way there will be total secrecy and no one spilling the beans.'

'It won't be easy cornering him,' Red Miller predicted. 'It could be weeks before the right opportunity comes up.'

'Ambrose likes walking,' Muiris pointed out. 'He spends a lot of time on the hill on his own. He told me once that lonely places are best for thinking deep, deep thoughts.'

'Is that a fact now?' Neil Durkin seemed to marvel.

'It's only to be expected,' Cormac reasoned. 'A murderer has a lot to think about, don't you know.'

'He's a rare murderer that doesn't get lonely in a lonely place,' Red Miller said.

'I've been out in all weathers and in all lights and I've often been on the hill and down the cliffs in the dead of night, and I never met anything worse than myself,' Muiris said. 'As my father used to say, what can't be seen by day can't be seen by night.'

'It's what you hear in the night that worries me,' Miller said. 'You hear noises in the dark that no man ever heard in broad daylight.'

'Whoever gets the Triangle needn't hurry,' Muiris assured them. 'He can take his time and choose the moment that suits him best. He can watch Ambrose's movements and get to know his habits. I've often caught a fox like that, by taking stock and working out his next move.'

Muiris went to the bedroom, and after ten minutes or so came back with five envelopes, which he put in the empty pail by the back door, just as he'd done before.

'You said we'd all swear secrecy on the Bible,' Miller reminded him.

'Well, would you believe it, there isn't a Bible in the house,' Muiris said with a glint of teeth. 'The nearest thing to a Bible is *Old Moore*.'

'You must have a missal or a prayer book, surely?' Miller said.

'Devil the one. I was never a great man for the books.'

In the absence of a prayer book of any kind, Muiris asked them to raise their right hand and repeat after him an oath

declaring never to reveal to anyone in court or out of it anything that had been said or done that evening. That seemed
to satisfy Miller who for reasons best known to himself was
deeply suspicious of his neighbours. Fortified and embold-
ened by Muiris's poteen, they all parted company around
midnight, each with an envelope in his jacket pocket.

13

Tom Barron was troubled. He couldn't think. He couldn't sleep. Nancy remarked that he was off his food and she wanted to know if he was feeling poorly. His response was to avoid the house in case she'd question him further. He spent the days on the hill tending the sheep and making sure his lambs stayed healthy. Usually, May was a favourite month because with new life came fresh ideas and plans. Not so this year. He could think of nothing but Ambrose and what Muiris and the others might do next. Though he tried his best, he could not shake off the weight of responsibility that kept deflecting the flow of his thoughts. He observed Ambrose's comings and goings. Sometimes he ran into him on the hill. Ambrose would smile a greeting and enquire about the sheep. With genuine interest in their welfare, he suggested once or twice that he wouldn't mind having a few ewes and lambs of his own.

One afternoon on the hill he saw Daniel coming towards him up the slope. Like Ambrose, he went walking for air and exercise and to allow his thoughts to wander freely after a morning's reading. Tom liked the schoolmaster. He was a sensible, no-nonsense man who didn't beat about the bush but came straight out with whatever was on his mind. He sat on a rock and filled his pipe as he watched Daniel's approach. They talked for a while about how cold it was at night for the time of year. Daniel said that his father always claimed that there was nothing worse for lambs than a wet, cold May.

Their joints would swell and it would take them a long time to recover, if they ever did. Tom said that he'd had no trouble so far. Though the weather was cold, it was mainly dry.

'I see you thatched the barn,' Daniel said.

'Ambrose gave me a hand. We did it in a while of a morning and an afternoon.'

'I'm worried about Ambrose,' Daniel said. 'After that meeting I didn't know what to think. I couldn't get him out of my mind.'

'I was worried about him, too. In fact, I'm still worried.'

'You mean he could still be in danger?'

'I don't know. Not knowing makes you imagine the worst. I didn't go to the last meeting, you see.'

'That's still going on, is it?'

'It could be. You know Muiris. Once he gets the bit between his teeth, he'll stop at nothing.'

'It would be terrible if anything happened to Ambrose. We'd never be able to forgive ourselves. Things would never be the same in Leaca again.'

'Trouble is, it's difficult to know what to do.'

'We could talk to him. Make him see the danger,' Daniel suggested.

'I've already advised him to get himself a real job in Dublin. I even told him Jim might be able to help.'

'Did you tell him the ghastly truth?'

'No, I didn't. He wouldn't have believed me. And even if he did, he wouldn't know what to do or what to think.'

'He could go back to England.'

'He's a headstrong man. Besides, he says he likes it here.'

'The alternative is for us to go to the police.'

'We don't have any real proof of a plot. Muiris and the others would deny it all. We'd only make a laughing-stock of ourselves.'

'So there's nothing we can do?' Daniel stared at the grass between his feet.

'We can keep a weather eye out for trouble. It's all we can do without causing bad blood among neighbours.'

He felt better for having talked to Daniel. For one thing he now knew that there was someone else who thought as he did, that he wasn't entirely alone.

He woke in darkness and realised that he would have to get up to make water. It was a nuisance that was happening to him more and more often. The doctor said that he himself had the same problem. He called it 'old man's disease'. Quietly, he stole out of bed so as not to disturb Nancy. The clock said ten past three. In the kitchen he pulled on his boots and put an old overcoat over his shoulders. Silently, he unbolted the back door and let himself out. He went round behind the old house and listened to the quiet flow of his water. It was a great relief. The flow ended but still he waited, knowing from experience that it could start again, this time little more than a dribble. He raised his head and saw the dark figure of a man steal past the corner. The man was standing by the kitchen window with his back to him. He seemed to be trying to open the window with something like a chisel. Tom reached for an old shovel shaft that stood against the barn wall and stole up behind him. He raised the shaft and brought it down on the intruder's head. The man groaned and slumped to the ground.

The first thought that occurred to Tom was that he might have hit him too hard. He gripped him under the arms and lugged him round to the back door. Opening the door, he dragged the unresisting deadweight into the kitchen. He struck a match and recognised the stubbled face of Ambrose. His eyes were closed but he was still breathing. He could come round at any minute, and in a tussle he was bound to come out best. He lit the oil-lamp and bound his arms and legs with a length of rope. Nancy came out of the bedroom and put both hands to her face.

'What terrible thing have you done, Tom?'

'He was trying to break into the house. I got him in the nick of time.'

'You killed him, Tom. What on earth will we do?'

'He'll come round in a minute. You go back to bed. I won't be long.'

'What are you going to do with him?'

'The law can deal with him. I'll put him on the cart and take him to the barracks first thing in the morning.'

When Nancy had gone back to bed, he gave Ambrose a couple of sharp slaps on the cheek. He grimaced and looked about him in alarm.

'My head,' he said. 'What happened?'

'I caught you trying to break into my house.'

Ambrose looked up at him, making a desperate effort to move his arms and legs.

'I must have been sleepwalking again,' he said.

'You mean you've done it before?'

'Sharon is worried. She's afraid I may fall down the cliffs one night.'

'You expect me to believe that?'

'You can ask her if you like.'

'I think you should tell your story to Sergeant McNally. He may believe you or he may not.'

'No, don't take me to the Sergeant. Let me go this once. I'll never do it again, I promise.'

'I'm going to put you in the old house for the night. It will give you a chance to come up with a better excuse. Don't call out and don't try to escape. If you do, you'll be in deep, deep trouble, let me tell you.'

He dragged Ambrose out to the barn and left him lying on the flagged floor.

'You can't leave me here all night, not in this freezing cold.'

'Don't worry, you'll survive.'

He bolted the barn door from the outside and hurried back to bed. As he expected, Nancy was still awake. She was a worrier was Nancy. He could tell that she had been praying.

'I put him in the barn till morning. I suppose we'd better try to get some sleep now.'

She had no intention of letting him sleep. She came up with one question after another. It took him a good half-hour to set her mind at rest. He lay on his back, breathing heavily, pretending to have dropped off. After a while he heard her even breathing and he knew that she had gone off. He himself did not expect to sleep. There was a flurry of excitement in his veins, which he took to be his blood coursing. He put his hand on his heart to see if it were pounding. It was beating at its normal rate.

'I shouldn't get excited,' he told himself. 'I should keep calm and try to work things out.'

He had assured Nancy that he would take Ambrose to the barracks in the morning but the more he thought about it the more convinced he became that it was not the sensible course of action. More than likely McNally would let him off with a warning. Even if he charged him with attempted burglary, he would have to release him pending trial. Ambrose would still be in danger from the Triangle, because Muiris and the others would now be fully convinced of his guilt. What if Muiris was right? What if Ambrose really was the murderer? He could have broken into Paddy Canty's house with nothing but Paddy's money on his mind. Quite possibly Paddy heard a noise and made the mistake of getting out of bed to investigate. It was all quite simple, or was it? The terrible thing was that he could not be sure. No one, except Ambrose, knew the truth. He thought about that simple fact for at least an hour. He himself would have to winkle the truth out of him, get him to sign a statement that he could present to McNally. It seemed quite straightforward. It was a wonder no one had thought of it before. The first driblets of daylight were leaking through the curtains when finally he fell asleep.

As usual, Nancy woke before him. 'I didn't get a wink of sleep,' she said. 'I kept dreaming all night about a stranger. Not Ambrose, but a tall dark stranger with a big fierce dog that frightened the life out of everyone in Leaca.'

'You're lucky to have such exciting dreams,' he said. 'I never dream. The minute I close my eyes my mind goes blank.'

Over breakfast she said, 'You'll be going to the barracks straight away. While you're in the village, you could get me a pan loaf and a pound of tea.'

'I won't be going to the village. Not today. I spent the night turning things over in my mind. I'll question Ambrose myself. If he's guilty, I'll get him to sign a confession.'

'But how will you know he's guilty?'

'I'll keep at him till I wear him down.'

'But that's a job for the guards!'

'And a fine job they've been making of it so far.'

He did not like having secrets he could not share with her. Obviously, he could not tell her the real reason he was holding Ambrose, which was to protect him from Muiris and the Triangle.

'I think you must be mad, Tom. His wife will go to the barracks and report him missing. The guards will be looking everywhere. They're bound to find him here.'

'You have a higher opinion of the guards than the rest of us,' he said.

Ambrose raised his head as he opened the barn door. He had a hangdog look, the look of a man who knew he was in no position to call the shots.

'I've got a cramp in my leg and it's killing me,' he said. 'I thought you'd never come.'

'I'll get you an old mattress to lie on. It will be more comfortable than the floor.'

'Enough is enough. You've had your little joke at my expense. If you let me go now, I'll say no more about it. It will be entirely between ourselves.'

'I won't be letting you go, not yet. Not till you've answered a few questions.'

'You can't hold me here! I know my rights! It's against the law!'

'And it's also against the law to break into another man's house.'

'I didn't break into your house.'

'You were trying to when I caught you.'

'It's your word against mine. There isn't an iota of proof against me.'

'We'll see about that.'

He closed the barn door and bolted it. Ambrose began shouting his head off. He opened the door and told him to shut up. He got a strip of old ticking and gagged him. Then he closed the door and bolted it again. He would allow him to simmer down. Give him time to realise that it was in his interest to co-operate.

Two hours later he went back to the old house. He laid a disused mattress on the floor and hauled Ambrose on to it. He placed a pillow under his head and removed the gag from his mouth.

'I'm willing to call it quits if you are,' Ambrose said. 'I'll just go about my business as usual and I won't say a thing to a soul.'

'What is your business? That's what I aim to find out.'

'You're a sensible man, Tom. You know you can't hold me here. If you do, you'll be breaking the law.'

'I'll let you go on one condition. You must first tell me the truth.'

'Of course, I'll tell you the truth. What do you want to know?'

'Why were you trying to break into my house last night?'

'I've already told you. I must have been sleepwalking.'

'I don't believe you. I've heard of people sleepwalking in the house but never outside the house, and not on a freezing cold night.'

'You're wrong there. Some sleepwalkers have been known to walk miles in the dark.'

'If you were sleepwalking, why were you in your working clothes?'

'I usually sleep in my pyjamas. I must have got up and dressed in my dream.'

'You were carrying a cold chisel. I suppose you picked it up on the way here, or was it part of your dream as well'?

'I'll admit to owning a bolster. I didn't know I had it on me. Quite possibly, in my dream I brought it along as a weapon of defence.'

'But why would you need to defend yourself if you didn't have badness in mind?'

'There's a murderer on the loose in Leaca. Like everyone else here, I feel vulnerable in the dark hours. Muiris has a gun. I've got a bolster. Is there anything wrong with that?'

'There's a big difference between you and Muiris. I didn't catch him trying to break into my house at three o'clock in the morning.'

'Well, of course not. As far as we know, Muiris isn't given to sleepwalking.'

'You have an answer for everything. The problem is that it isn't the right answer.'

'I've told you the truth. Now will you let me go?'

'You're in for the long haul, me bucko. You're here and you'll remain here till you begin talking sense.'

'Tell me what you want me to say and I'll say it, if that's what pleases you.'

'Mockery will get you nowhere. The sooner you realise I'm serious, the sooner you'll get out of here. As far as I'm concerned, you're here till you tell the truth, however long it takes. I'll get you your breakfast now. You might make more sense on a full stomach.'

He asked Nancy to boil an egg, and butter three slices of soda bread to go with it.

'He likes his eggs hard-boiled,' she said. 'I'd better leave it on for nine minutes.'

'He's hard-boiled enough already. A soft-boiled egg might do him the world of good.'

'What did he say?'

'He'd like me to think he was sleepwalking last night.'

'Well, maybe he was.'

'And I suppose I was sleepwalking when I caught him.'

'That makes two of you, two headstrong men.'

'I don't really care what he was up to last night. What I really want to know is whether he murdered poor Paddy.'

'You're taking too much on yourself, Tom. You're not the law, you have no authority. I know you mean well, but in the eyes of the law you're just like any ordinary man.'

'If I were any ordinary man, I'd take him to the barracks. That's the easy way out.'

'Can't you see it's the right way, Tom?'

'The right way was never the easy way. If it was, we'd all be saints.'

'I know in my heart you're wrong, Tom. Listen to me for once and let him go.'

He didn't like being what she called 'headstrong'. On most things they'd always seen eye to eye. He watched as she took a tablespoon from the dresser and lifted the egg from the saucepan. She put the egg in an eggcup and placed it beside the buttered bread on a plate. He found the sequence of simple actions reassuring; it seemed to confirm that it was just another ordinary day.

'My mind's adrift,' she said. 'I clean forgot to make his tea. Maybe you should take him the egg before it gets cold.'

'Don't worry. A cold egg is as good as a warm one. I was often glad of a cold egg cutting turf on the bog.'

Ambrose gave him a sullen look as he entered. Obviously, he had come to realise that this wasn't just a game.

'I've brought your breakfast. We'll talk after you've eaten.'

'It isn't breakfast I need but a doctor. My head feels split down the middle. I think I may be suffering from brain damage.'

'Is that why you can't tell the truth?'

'I'm serious. I need a doctor right away.'

'You know I can't get you a doctor. When you've eaten, I'll have a look at your head myself.'

'You're not a doctor. You know nothing about concussion. If anything happens to me, you'll be had up for manslaughter or worse.'

'Pipe down and eat your breakfast.'

'How can I eat bound hand and foot?'

'That's no problem. I'll feed you like a baby.'

'I won't be spoon-fed. I'm going on hunger strike till you release me.'

'Stubbornness will get you nowhere. You'll come round in time, don't worry. There's nothing like an empty stomach to make a man see someone else's point of view.'

As he put the gag back on, he felt the scalp with his fingertips. The skin wasn't broken. As far as he could judge, there was nothing the matter with him that time wouldn't cure on its own. He closed the door with a bang, driving the bolt home with the full force of his arm.

'He's being awkward,' he told Nancy. 'He's refusing to eat.'

'He isn't being awkward, Tom, he's being clever. He knows that if he goes on hunger strike, you'll have to release him because you wouldn't want a death on your conscience.'

'If he thinks I'm a softie, he's in for a surprise.'

'He's cleverer than you are. Mark my words, he'll get the better of you, Tom.'

'You must have a very poor opinion of me, so.'

'No, I don't. I just always know when you're going too far.'

He spent the rest of the morning on the hill. His mind wasn't on the sheep, however. He could only think about Nancy and what she had said. He respected her opinion. He didn't like having to disagree with her, but in the circumstances there was nothing else he could do. After a while his thoughts turned to Ambrose. He was proving awkward but he'd soon find out that the man he was dealing with was no daw. The refusal to eat was something he hadn't foreseen. Ambrose was just trying it on, of course. He was used to going hungry, but he'd soon cave in when the pangs got keen. In the meantime he'd keep a watchful eye on him. There was no hurry. Unlike Ambrose, he could afford to play a waiting game.

On the way home he met Sharon at the end of the lane.

'You haven't seen Nick by any chance?' she said.

'He isn't on the hill. If he were, I'd have seen him.'

'He got up early. He hasn't been back for breakfast. If you see him, perhaps you could tell him that Red Miller was looking for him. He was supposed to be giving him a hand with the turf-cutting today.'

'I'll do that,' he said. 'It's a busy time of year. I could do with a helping hand myself.'

She smiled as she turned away. She was good-looking but nervous. She kept touching her hair and glancing upwards as she talked, which made him feel uneasy. Daniel said she was never at ease except in front of her easel. Daniel knew about painting. He said she was a better artist than Ambrose was a writer; that he was only good for pinching other people's ideas. They were an odd couple. Neil Durkin, who was their nearest neighbour, said they fought some nights like Kilkenny cats.

14

*T*om Barron was a sound man. He was Nick's favourite neighbour. Talking to him had helped clear Sharon's mind, not because of anything he'd said but because of the way he had of talking. It wasn't an intimate way of saying things; it was long distance, as if an ocean lay between him and you. Earlier, she had felt confused and uncertain. Now she could see what must be done. She had missed him from the bed around three, and she must have lain awake for at least an hour, wondering where he'd gone. Then she fell asleep again and didn't wake till after seven. When he still hadn't come back, she became worried. It was the second time he'd left the house in the middle of the night.

The first time was the night Paddy Canty was murdered. On that occasion he came back two hours later, barely able to talk. The following day he swore black and blue that he'd had nothing to do with the murder, and she had given him the benefit of the doubt. Now she wasn't so sure. There was only one explanation for his disappearance. He had obviously done a bunk, having realised that the law was closing in on him. Red Miller had been enquiring about him. Soon word would get around that he'd absconded, and she would be in trouble for not having reported him missing. She took Emily by the hand and went over to Daniel Burke's.

'You haven't seen Nick by any chance?' she said.

'Not since yesterday. He said he'd be working for Red Miller today.'

'Well, he isn't with Miller. I was wondering where he could have gone. You see, he hasn't been home all day.'

'Didn't he say where he was going?' Daniel asked.

'He was missing from the bed when I woke this morning. We had a row last night, I'm afraid. At first I thought he'd gone off in a huff and that he'd be back after an hour or two when he'd simmered down. It's now nearly six and he still hasn't turned up.'

'Maybe you should tell the guards.'

'Well, I don't want to do anything stupid. He left in a huff once before when we were living in Dublin, but he came back the following day.'

'Leave it till tomorrow, then. If he doesn't turn up in the meantime, I'll run you down to the barracks in the morning.'

That night she went to bed without bolting the door, thinking he might come back. She woke up in the middle of the night and put over her hand out of habit, but his half of the bed was cold. The possibility that he might not be coming back hit her like a fist in the face.

It had been a long night. It was freezing in the barn. The cold had seeped through his body to the very marrow of his bones. He felt terrible. His head was on fire, and his arms and legs screamed out in protest against the ropes that bound them. He could live with physical pain. What he could not endure was not knowing what Sharon was doing, where she was, what she was thinking and what her next move might be. If only they hadn't had that row. Now she would jump to the wrong conclusion and think he'd walked out on her. Of course, it wasn't their first row. She was short-tempered and so was he. Their past relationship had been punctuated by rows, most of them over silly things like whether she should go to Dublin on her own. He had offered to go with her more than once, but she always said he'd only be in the way.

She was going to Dublin to sell her paintings, and that was something she preferred to do on her own. She didn't need a minder. She was well able to look after herself.

It wasn't that simple. She'd be seeing Paul Flynn, and he knew and she knew that Flynn still had his eye on her. Flynn fancied himself as a ladies' man, and Sharon might be tempted to please him for the sake of an editorial mention. Flynn was good-looking and amusing. He liked a drink and so did Sharon. Once, when Nick told her to be on her guard, she said, 'What do you take me for, a schoolgirl?' That started it. She refused to speak to him for two whole days.

They'd had good times together in Dublin, living in a cheap flat in Sandymount with a window at the back looking out on the Dodder. They had one bicycle between them; they went everywhere and did everything together. Their great friend in those days was Brendan Hurley, who was teaching maths and physics at Trinity while he put the finishing touches to his PhD thesis. Brendan lived with his sister in Ballsbridge, a short walk from their flat. They used to meet in Crowe's and then take a bus to the quays. Brendan was an omnivorous reader, and because of his scientific background he had things to say about art and literature that would never have occurred to a student of the humanities. Sharon said that he had a highly original mind; that his only fault was his emotional dependence on his sister Delma. He told her that he'd never marry, and that he shared a flat with Delma because she never made any demands that he could not satisfy.

One evening Brendan introduced them to a journalist called Paul Flynn, who worked for the *Irish Press*. Flynn was young and carefree, an inventive conversationalist who was never short of a bob or two. He had a well-stocked mind. He talked to Nick about literature and to Sharon about art. Sharon said that he was a good man to know. Soon she was looking up to him as a kind of mentor. She invited him to the flat to look at her paintings and discussed with him what she was planning to do next. It was Flynn who said that as an artist what she needed was exposure to 'the elemental experi-ence' and that the best place to find it was on the west coast of Ireland. He himself had spent a summer in a place called Leaca learning Irish as a boy. It was a summer he would never forget.

'You really must go,' he said. 'It will be the making of you as an artist, and I'm sure Nick will find some useful raw mate-rial as well.' Why did Flynn suggest Leaca if he had his eye on her? Perhaps he was trying to cover up for something. He himself had no objection to trying out Leaca, even though the suggestion had come from Flynn.

As things turned out, he took to the people like a duck to water. It was Sharon who found them heavy going. After the first week she said that she had no idea what Flynn could have been thinking of, that he'd deliberately given them a wrong steer. Nick knew better than to believe her. She never went to Dublin without getting in touch with Flynn. He was her art guru and father confessor. For all he knew Flynn could be consoling her now. He disliked having to think about him. Flynn was an unknown territory, like the dark side of the moon.

He rolled onto his back and tried to do some stretching exercises. Thinking about Sharon and Flynn would get him nowhere. The infuriating thing about her was that she saw herself as his superior. She was convinced that his stories did not sell because they were no good.

'The bones are there but where's the meat?' was how she'd put it. 'Every good writer has an argument and a char-acteristic point of view. When you think of Thomas Hardy, you think of the malevolence of fate; and when you think of Jane Austen, you think of an ironic wit.'

When he told her that what she called 'argument' was for journalists, polemicists and other simple souls, she accused him of vanity and wrong-headedness. He realised then that they would never see eye to eye on any literary matter. What irritated him above all else was that she had picked up the word 'argument' from Flynn. Quite possibly, they had discussed him behind his back on her last visit to Dublin. But what could you expect from someone whose favourite modern writer was George Orwell and whose favourite modern novel was *Animal Farm?* She tended to like books whose essence could be expressed in one short sentence. It was all a matter of 'reduction', she said, comparing the process to a cook 'reducing' the gravy. He suspected that she had picked up that idea from Flynn as well. He had told her that she and Flynn were both misguided dilettanti. Any story that was worth telling would resist all attempts at what she called 'reduction'. A good story could not be paraphrased without doing for its subtlety and complexity. You read it. You dwelt on it. You didn't try to convert it into something that it was not. He felt strongly about that. A story, he told her, was not a substance to be reduced by chemical process to a simpler form. Naturally, she did not understand. She would never be happy in Leaca, a place of stories, for that very reason. She was forever complaining about what she called the 'emptiness', whereas for him it was the ideal place in which to write a book about nothing, what Flaubert called *un livre sur rien*. She would never understand that in Leaca nothing wasn't nothing; the crooked timber of humanity lay all around. He had come into his own, he felt, and all Sharon could think of was going to Dublin to meet art critics at parties. Thinking about her would only make him angry. Instead he should be thinking about what to say to Tom Barron.

Tom wasn't like Muiris. He was the kind of man who would strive to do what was right. Quite obviously, he was convinced that he had murdered Paddy Canty. Somehow or other he would have to convince him of his innocence. There was one solid fact he could rely on. Tom had a sense of proportion. In pursuit of his objective, he would only go so far. By now he would be worried about his captive's decision to refuse food and water. He would know that no one could survive more than three or four days without a drink.

So it would be a matter of who gave in first. For him the test would be one of physical endurance; for Tom it was primarily moral. The outcome was difficult to call, if only because it was possible to endure moral discomfort for longer than enervating physical agony. But more than likely, Tom would be under pressure from Nancy who would be bound to tell him he'd gone too far. After all he hadn't broken into the house. The worst that could be said against him was that he had been acting suspiciously, and he had given a convincing explanation of how that had come about. He would stick to his story. Stories were part of the oral culture of Leaca, stories about neighbours alive and neighbours dead. People were used to telling and hearing the same stories over and over again. Tom Barron would not expect him to change his story. One of the features of a good story was that it became more real with each retelling.

He was probably being alarmist, thinking in terms of a prolonged ordeal. Tom might well release him before nightfall. Nancy would give him dinner and he would agree to say no more about the matter. Nancy was an inspired cook, given the limited ingredients at her disposal. She once gave him a dinner of bacon and fried cabbage that he would never forget. After making his peace with Tom he would go home and make peace with Sharon. Everything would return to normal, no questions asked.

He wasn't looking forward to working again with Red Miller, who was rough, ready and irascible. Besides, his wife was no cook. A month or two after their arrival in Leaca he'd spent two days helping him earth up his potatoes. They turned out to be the hardest two days of his life. Red Miller gave him an old spade with a short, worn-out blade and asked him to dig what he called the sheughs between the ridges while he himself did the earthing-up with a shovel. Miller worked like a demon, forcing Nick, who was on the ridge ahead of him, to work like a demon as well. Towards evening it turned to rain, but Red Miller took no notice. By dusk they were both soaking wet. Then Nick struck a hidden rock and broke the shaft of the spade. Red Miller wasn't best pleased.

'That was my grandfather's spade,' he said, 'and he was given it by his father. With a bit of care it would have seen me out as well.'

'The wood was decayed where it joined the metal. There, you can see for yourself.'

'I have a good mind to dock a shilling from your pay.'

'If you do, I'll never work for you again. The wood was rotten. It wasn't my fault.'

'That's what I like, a man who'll stand up for himself. Sure, I was only coddin'. I'll put a new shaft in her the next wet day. We'll eat now. There's nothing like a full belly after a good day's work.'

Nick didn't disagree. He felt disconsolate in his wet clothes. When they reached the house, Miller took two bottles of stout from the dresser. He poured one into a tumbler, which he handed to Nick, while he himself drank straight from the bottle.

'I like stout. When you drink it quickly from the bottle, the gas makes you burp, and if you're lucky, it will sting your nostrils and maybe bring a tear to your eye as well.'

Nick watched as Miller's wife busied herself about the kitchen, moving things unnecessarily and making a lot of noise. A big black pot hung over the turf fire and now and again the lid would lift as a spurt of steam escaped.

'Is supper nearly ready, Madge?' Red Miller asked. 'I could eat an ox, so I could.'

'It isn't ox you'll be getting but stirabout,' she said with a tilt of the head.

'Nothing better,' Red Miller burped. 'It's good for the bowels, it keeps you regular. They say a man could live on stirabout and nothing else.'

Madge put two small bowls and two spoons on the bare table. Between the bowls, she placed a jug of milk. Next she poured porridge from the pot into a large mixing bowl and placed it on the table next to the jug. Red Miller sat at the head of the table and motioned to Nick to take the only other chair. Madge sat alone on a creepie stool by the fire and began eating straight from the pot.

Red Miller was a noisy eater. He slurped and grunted, while rivulets of milk ran down his chin. The porridge was yellow and grainy like sand, but at least the milk was good.

'What do you think of the stirabout?' Red Miller asked.

'It's different. I've never had yellow porridge before.'

'It's Indian meal stirabout. If you eat enough of it, it will put a thick coat of hair on your chest.'

Nick was hungry. The porridge was piping hot and he cooled it with lashings of milk, keeping one eye on his host and the other on his wife, while thanking heavens that Red Miller's was like no other house in Leaca.

'Whereabouts in England do you come from?' Red Miller asked.

'Sussex. I was brought up on a farm near Rye.'

'My great grandfather came from Sheffield. I reckon I must be one-eighth English. You wouldn't think that now, would you?'

'After all this time you must be a hundred per cent Irish, I would say.'

'But I'm not a hundred per cent Leaca. The neighbours still see me as a foreigner. You could live here for ten generations and still be a stranger. You and me, we have more in common than you think.'

'I can't complain,' Nick said. 'The people here are friendly. They all stop to talk whenever I meet them on the road.'

'Fishing for news, that's their game. All flattery to your face, and they'd skin you alive when your back is turned. The only man in Leaca I'd trust is Tom Barron.'

'I get on with them all.'

'You'll live and learn the hard way,' Red Miller said. 'We English should stick together. Here, we're the odd men out.'

He gave Nick a playful punch on the shoulder that very nearly knocked him sideways.

He didn't relish the turn the conversation had taken. He told himself that if everyone in Leaca was like Red Miller, he wouldn't remain in the place another day. But with hindsight perhaps he should not have dismissed his opinion so readily. Red Miller had reason to know his neighbours. Maybe there was a granule of truth in what he'd been saying. He was wrong in saying Daniel didn't know his own mind, that he couldn't see a fence without sitting on it, but he was right in saying Muiris was as crooked as a corkscrew.

Footsteps in the yard alerted him. The bolt shot back and the door opened. Tom Barron was standing between him and the light. He removed the gag with a grunt.

'Have you had second thoughts yet?'

'Second thoughts about what?'

'Your sleepwalking story, what else?'

'I've told you the truth. It isn't my fault if you don't believe me.'

'I'm going to ask you another question. Think carefully before you answer it. Where were you the night Paddy Canty was murdered?'

'In my bed like you. I had nothing to do with it.'

'Are you sure you weren't walking in your sleep that night as well?'

'As sure as I'm talking to you now.'

'How can you be sure? A man who walks in his sleep doesn't know what he's doing. As I see it, this is what happened. You were sleepwalking when you tried to break into my house last night. You could also have been sleepwalking the night poor Paddy was murdered. You see what I mean? You do things in your sleep without knowing you're doing them.'

'A man can't be guilty of something he isn't conscious of doing. But all that's beside the point. I wasn't trying to break into your house and I didn't murder Paddy Canty.'

'You obviously haven't suffered enough. Only thirst and hunger will make you face the truth about yourself.'

He picked up the gag again and started to put it on.

'Just a minute. Can we talk?' He thought he might play for time.

'If you have something sensible to say, I'll listen.'

'Look, Tom, whenever we've had dealings, you've been fair. I'm telling you the truth but you don't believe me. I can't change what I say without telling a lie, and neither can you change what you believe to be true. It's the way you're made. In other words the truth I'm telling you doesn't correspond with your sense of reality.'

'Are you saying I'm too stupid to understand?'

'No, I meant that what I'm saying doesn't ring true to you.'

'You can say that again. This conversation is getting us nowhere.'

'You see what I mean? This situation won't change unless one of us does something or says something he doesn't believe in. But it can't go on indefinitely because after another day I'll be too weak from hunger and thirst to make sense. It's the classic situation: an irresistible force meets an immovable object.'

'You're using big words but they don't fool me. I never use a word that doesn't mean what I mean.'

'I'm being serious, Tom. If you hold me here without food and water for much longer, you'll have my death on your conscience.'

'No, I won't. If you want to commit suicide, it's entirely up to you,' he said, putting on the gag.

He could see that he was angry because he'd lost the argument. He was an intelligent man was Tom. He would now go away and think it over. He might even discuss it with Nancy. The thought gave him hope. Next time he came, he would suggest that he get an arbiter to decide between them.

The effort of speaking had weakened him. His throat hurt and the sides of his stomach ached as if a family of rodents was gnawing at them. He closed his eyes and tried to think of something else. He remembered a story Muiris had told him about Fionn Mac Cumhaill and the salmon of knowledge. It was the most enchanting story he'd ever heard but, like the story he'd told Tom Barron, it challenged one's sense of verisimilitude. Everyone in Leaca knew the story of Fionn and the salmon, and they believed it to be true, but only in a sense. There were degrees of belief and different forms of belief. He would have to think about that in relation to Tom Barron.

15

She'd had a sleepless night, listening for a step in the yard and the sound of the latch being lifted quietly. 'Quietly' was a word she associated with Nick. He was big-boned and strong, but he wasn't rough. If anything, he seemed excessively conscious of the comparative fragility of other people. His lovemaking was passionate but tender. Unlike some of the men she'd known, he wasn't a bull in a china shop. It was unlike him to leave her here on her own. In Dublin she would have had friends to turn to. Here there was no one to confide in, and that was something he would have realised. They had a strong relationship in spite of their quarrels; he couldn't conceivably have walked out on her.

Luckily, she had four finished paintings to sell. She would take them to Dublin, and while in Dublin she'd see Brendan Hurley. It was a strange relationship. On her trips they always met in Crowe's because that was where they'd met the first time. They had had a drink or two, after which he invited her back to his flat for 'soup and a crust'. Soup and a crust—that was how he'd put it, leading her to think at the time that he was the most scatty and unworldly man she'd ever met. He gave her mulligatawny from a tin and they shared his only roll. Then they sat together on the sofa, listening to chamber music on the radio and talking about his sister Delma who'd gone out for the evening.

'Come and sit here,' he said. 'I'm curious to see what it's like to have the weight of a girl on my knee.'

She laughed because she thought him naive. She sat on his knee and playfully pulled the lobe of his ear.

'You've got very bony knees,' she said to tease him. 'They're biting into my bum.'

'Isn't that a shame now, and you as light as a feather? Sure, you're no weight at all. I'd never get tired of your lightness pressing. It's as if you're about to float off into the air.'

He kissed her on the neck and then he kissed her on the lips. One thing led to another in a series of actions that seemed entirely innocent and undesigning. She'd lost all sense of place and time. She could think of nothing but the moment; and the moment, of course, demanded the somnolence of present fulfilment. It should never have happened.

'I'm afraid I got carried away.' She pulled down her dress over her knees.

'Me, too. You won't mention it to Nick,' he said.

'Even if I did, he wouldn't believe me. You see, he's obsessed with Paul Flynn to the exclusion of every other man. Whenever I come back from Dublin, he asks me if I've seen him. He calls you Bernard but he calls Paul Flynn just Flynn. That's the difference. He's obsessed with Paul, I think.'

'Now, isn't that the good one. Paul is fond of Nick. He was talking about him in the pub only last night.'

On the way home she told herself that it must not happen again. She liked Brendan. She found his company relaxing but she would never fall in love with him, because she knew in her heart that she couldn't desert Nick. The very contrariety of things conspired against her, however. It was as if there were an infernal law saying that what had happened once must happen again and again with a regularity that robbed the action of either spontaneity or design. The very thought of it filled her with a sense of diminishment. She pulled on her coat over her dress and took Emily by the hand.

'We're going to see Daniel and Sheila,' she said.

Sheila was knitting a sock and Daniel was reading a book. She liked Daniel but she was wary of Sheila because she sensed that Sheila saw her as a flibbertigibbet who might conceivably set her husband's thoughts astray. She had a big, bland, expressionless face and, as if that wasn't enough, she kept Daniel on the shortest of leads. They went everywhere and did everything together, in contravention of the local custom by which men spent their time with other men in the fields while their womenfolk confined themselves to the house. It was nothing short of tragic to see a good man so henpecked.

Sheila pretended to smile as she dusted a chair for her. She didn't offer Emily a chair; she obviously expected her to stand.

'Sorry to barge in on you like this. Nick still hasn't come home. I'm afraid something may have happened to him. I suppose I should tell the police.'

'Sure, what could have happened to him?' Sheila said.

'He likes going for walks on the cliffs. He could have fallen down a bank. We just don't know.'

'I'll give you a lift to the barracks,' Daniel said. 'It will save you shoe leather, if nothing else.'

'And I'll come as well,' Sheila put aside her knitting. 'I need a few things from the shop.'

She had been hoping to talk to Daniel alone but it was not to be. Sheila sat in the passenger seat, while she sat with Emily in the back. Daniel didn't say much; he allowed Sheila to do the talking, and though he'd probably heard it all before, he showed no sign of boredom. Sharon wondered how an intelligent man could put up with her. Sheila was the most tedious woman she'd ever met.

'Are we going to see Daddy?' Emily asked.

'He'll be home soon, darling. Promise Mummy you'll be patient, now will you?'

Sergeant McNally was a friendly man. Rumour had it that he had a glad eye for the ladies when his wife wasn't around. He smiled at her as she sat down.

'It's about Nick,' she said. 'He wasn't in the bed when I woke up yesterday morning, and he still hasn't come home.'

'You mean he's gone missing?'

'I'm afraid something may have happened to him. He could have fallen down a cliff in the dark.'

'Or skedaddled, more like! Now that's very inconvenient. I was planning to have another word with him today. You say he's been missing since yesterday morning?'

'That's right.'

'He's had a twenty-four hour start on us, but don't worry, we'll catch up with him. We'll put a watch on all the ports. He's unlikely to escape by air.'

'I think you're jumping to conclusions, Sergeant. He may have had an accident; he may be in need of help.'

'You can leave all that to me. I'll get in touch with you as soon as any hard information comes to hand.'

It was hopeless talking to him. She got up and put an arm round Emily.

'I think you should mount a search of the coast, Sergeant.'

'First things first. I'll come to that, if need be.'

'It looks bad,' Sheila said on the way home. 'Imagine just walking out on you like that. I don't know what I'd do if Daniel did it to me.'

She didn't respond. She felt bruised and helpless. She sat clutching Emily's hand and looked out of the window at a harsh, inhospitable landscape of scree, bracken and scant heather. What on earth could have brought her here? She must have been dreaming at the time.

'What did he say?' Nancy asked.

'He's sticking to his story, he refuses to budge.'

'Why do you keep calling it "his story"? He could be telling the truth.'

'Well of course he isn't. Who ever heard of a man walking three hundred yards on a rough road in his sleep? Besides, he was wearing his working clothes. If he'd just got out of bed, he'd be barefoot in his semmit and long johns.'

'You have an answer for everything, Tom, that's your trouble.'

'He's a contrary man. He won't eat and he won't drink, and he won't change his tune.'

'That makes two of you. He's no more contrary than you are.'

'Well, he can't hold out much longer.'

'He'll run rings round you, Tom. He knows you well enough to know you won't let him die.'

'Well, maybe he's mistaken. Tom Barron is no softie.'

'Look, Tom, I have an idea. We'll kill the black hen that isn't laying. We'll have her for supper tonight with potatoes and turnips. I have some pearl barley left over from Christmas. It will help to make good thick soup.'

'What are you talking about?'

'We'll lay the table for three. You'll bring him in here when it's ready. Once he gets the smell of soup, he'll see sense.'

'You must be out of your mind, Nancy?'

'I'll put on the kettle and we'll have a cup of tea and talk about it.'

In her quiet way she was very headstrong, and over the years she'd turned out to be right more than once. He watched her going about the kitchen for a while. Then he picked up the local paper and turned the pages, just reading the headlines because he couldn't read the small print without his glasses. He'd already made up his mind. He needed to talk to another man, and Daniel was the only one who fitted the bill.

He was a man of habit, was Daniel. Tom made sure to be on the cliffs in time for his mid-afternoon walk. He sat on a rock and watched four cormorants stretching their wings on the Stuaic. The sea was as grey as the sky, and the bay seemed calm enough in spite of the white run about the rocks. He charged his pipe as he waited for the schoolmaster to come up. They talked for a bit about the bogs and whether they were dry enough for the turf-cutting.

'It's the frost that worries me,' Tom said. 'We had frost in May two years ago. A heavy frost will ruin the best of turf.'

'Did you hear about Ambrose?' Daniel said after a while. 'Sharon says she hasn't seen him since Tuesday. I gave her a lift to the barracks this morning. The police are putting a watch on all the ports.'

'So they think he hoisted sail and left?'

'All I know is that McNally wants to question him again.'

'Can you keep a secret, Daniel?'

'You don't mean to say he's fallen victim to the Triangle?'

'No, I don't mean that. This is something only I know about, and I can't tell you unless you promise not to mention it to anyone, not even Sheila.'

'Well, it must be something terrible, so.'

'Do you promise?'

Daniel thought for a moment.

'You can tell me,' he said. 'I won't say a word to anyone.'

'Tuesday night I got up around three to make my water. My bladder isn't what it used to be, I'm afraid. Well, I went out behind the barn and who did I find trying to break into the house but my bold Ambrose. I knew it was either him or me, so I picked up an old shovel shaft and hit him over the head with it. I tied him up and left him in the barn for the night, thinking I'd take him to the barracks in the morning. But after all the excitement I couldn't get back to sleep, so I got to thinking. If I take him to the barracks, he'll get off with a warning because I can't prove anything; and if he gets off, his life will be in even more danger from the Triangle. So what was I to do? I decided to keep him in the old house for a day or two until he confessed to Paddy's murder, thinking I'd succeed where the guards failed. Then I'd hand him over to McNally with the signed confession. It seemed straightforward and sensible at the time but, would you believe it, he's refusing to budge. He won't eat and he won't drink and he won't admit he did it. So I'm in a bit of a pickle, Daniel. I don't want to give in, but nor do I want a death on my hands.'

'It's a tricky one.' Daniel plucked a stalk of mountain grass from the clump at his feet and began chewing the white butt.

Tom re-lit his pipe as he waited for him to continue. He looked down at the cormorants on the Stuaic, now reduced to three, all of them facing out to sea.

'To be honest, I don't know what I should do,' he said finally between puffs of the pipe.

'Maybe you should sleep on it,' Daniel advised.

'Sleep on it? I can't sleep. I haven't had a good night's sleep since all this began.'

'If you're building a house, you don't start with the chimney. You build from the foundations up.'

'What does that mean?' Tom betrayed more than a hint of irritation.

'Well, you assumed from the start that he's guilty. You started with the chimney, I'm afraid.'

'But I caught him red-handed! He was trying to break into my house.'

'And you assumed, therefore, that he murdered Paddy Canty. It doesn't add up.'

'You think I'm wrong, then?'

'You may be right, of course, but you can't depend on it.'

'So what should I do?'

'I think you should take him to the barracks and tell your story to McNally. You may be in trouble for depriving him of his liberty for two whole days but that's better than having his death on your conscience.'

'A man who goes to law can have no idea where it all will end. I've never stood inside a courtroom; I've always solved my own problems in my own way.'

'The law has its uses,' Daniel said. 'It has the force of right behind it.'

'If McNally says Ambrose has no case to answer, he'll still be in danger from the Triangle when he's released. Then I'll have his death on my conscience anyway, and so will you.'

'You won't be directly implicated and neither will I. It will happen at one remove away. That's different from allowing an innocent man in your care to die of thirst and hunger.'

'It wouldn't be murder but suicide—death by his own decision.'

'You could be had up for manslaughter.'

'Look, Daniel. Ambrose is an educated man and so are you. If you talk to him, he'll listen to you. He doesn't take me seriously, he thinks I'm a simpleton, you see.'

'What can I say to him that you haven't said already?'

'It isn't what you say; it's how you say it. You know how to put things. A word from your mouth will mean more than ten from mine.'

'As I see it, it wouldn't make a ha'p'orth of difference. You don't know Ambrose. He sees himself as an artist with a mission. In his thinking he's as hard as flint stone. He probably sees all this as a test of his integrity. If he's innocent, he won't budge.'

He could see that Daniel didn't want to get involved. He was a thinking man who could take in the consequences of any action at a glance.

'You feel he's innocent, then?'

'That's how it looks to me.'

'And that's your final word?'

'I'm sorry, Tom. I can't help you with this one. It's a mile beyond my reach.'

Tom knocked out his pipe on the toecap of his boot. One of the cormorants was pecking at the shoulder of the bird next to her.

'How long can a man last without food and water?

'He'll last longer without food than he would without water. I would say that three days without water would test any man. Of course, it may depend to some extent on the temperature. He won't sweat much in this weather.'

'Three days, you say? I've only one day left.'

'If I were you, I'd take him to the barracks. This problem is too big for any man to handle alone.'

'Maybe you're right.'

Tom got up and stood looking out at the horizon, which had melted into the sky, or perhaps the sky had melted into the sea. The boundaries between things were vanishing before his eyes. The cormorants had gone. The Stuaic was bare.

'Strange how cormorants come and go without rhyme or reason!' He seemed to be talking to himself.

'There were three of them on the Stuaic just now, but something must have frightened them,' Daniel said. 'They took off for Bud a' Diabhail, one after the other.'

'They're the devil's own bird, so they are. They're good for nothing but eating and shitting.' The vehemence of his voice surprised him.

'I wouldn't mind having their capacity to withstand cold.'

'Sure, gulls and gannets are the same. Maybe what we all need is a coat of feathers.'

'Soon it will be time for the lobster fishing,' Daniel said.

'You'll come out with us one evening. By then all this will be over.'

'I'll look forward to that.'

He watched as Daniel continued on his walk, his right arm swinging and his left hand in his trousers pocket. Some days he went north, others south. Today he was heading south for the Tower. He was a good man, was Daniel, but he agonised over every little thing. Unlike Muiris, he was too scrupulous to be strong.

That evening Muiris invited the men of the townland, apart from Daniel and Tom Barron, to a meeting. By nine o'clock they'd all arrived, except Red Miller, whose cow had just calved. Muiris poured drinks even more generously than usual, and they all seemed to drink with greater gusto than usual. Relaxing in their seats like a theatre audience before the curtain goes up, they talked about the approaching lobster season. Everyone knew what was on everyone else's mind, but they were all leaving it to Muiris to broach the one and only subject.

'Red Miller doesn't let the grass grow under his feet. The news about Ambrose surprised even me,' Muiris said finally.

'It was very sudden.' Cormac put on a serious face.

'It had to be sudden,' his friend Marcus reminded them.

'You're right,' said Muiris. 'A bolt from the blue. It's the divine nature of the act.'

'The nature of the beast,' Neil Durkin corrected.

'Still, it's strange to think we'll never see him again,' Cormac mused.

Red Miller arrived at ten. Muiris pulled up a chair for him and gave him the full glass of poteen he'd already poured in readiness.

'Was it a heifer calf?' he asked.

'No, a fine bull calf.' Red Miller pursed his lips.

'The arse fell out of the market for bull calves years ago,' Muiris remarked.

'You can say that again,' Cormac nodded. 'Sure, you can't give bull calves away these days.'

'He'll make good veal in two months' time,' Red Miller said seriously. 'He's good for nothing else.'

'We should look at the bright side,' Muiris advised. 'With Ambrose gone, we can all sleep sound in our beds again. It's a job that had to be done, and now that it's done, it's well done.'

'It's all a great mystery,' Neil Durkin remarked. 'Only one man knows how he met his end and where his bones are resting.'

'And that's how it should be. A secret is a secret. We won't enquire. If no one knows, no one can spill the beans.' Muiris raised his hand, as if to emphasise finality.

'It's a story without an ending, and that's a pity,' Neil Durkin said. 'Whoever tells it when we're gone will have to make up an ending.'

'Ending or no ending, he was a great nuisance,' Cormac said. 'I lost enough turf from the shed to keep any house going for the longest winter.'

'What will we do now with all the extra turnips, potatoes and eggs?' Marcus Quinn wondered.

'None of those things mattered,' Muiris said. 'What matters is that Paddy can rest in peace now that justice is finally done. So let's drink to his memory.'

'To Paddy,' they all echoed, before draining their glasses.

Muiris poured more poteen for everyone except himself. As was his custom, he partook of a hot whiskey with extra cloves and sugar.

'I ran into the Sergeant in Cashel this afternoon,' he said. 'He's putting a watch on all the ports.'

'Well, isn't that a good one,' Cormac smiled.

'Little does he know.' Marcus Quinn looked at Red Miller, who looked down into his glass.

'The things that go on behind a man's back!' Neil Durkin slapped his thigh.

'I told him not to forget the airports,' Muiris said. '"We must make sure the bastard is caught," says I.'

Muiris exposed his teeth in silent laughter as his lower jaw trembled uncontrollably. Neil Durkin slapped his thigh again, and Cormac said, 'Well, that's the best I ever heard.'

They all looked a bit flushed, or perhaps it was just the firelight playing on their cheeks. Gradually, they became serious as their conversation returned to practical, everyday things. Lobster creels had to be repaired in readiness for the new season, covers knitted and byan nets darned. And to cap it all, this year's turf had to be cut and won.

'There's no rest for the wicked,' Cormac said.

'No rest at all,' his friend Marcus Quinn agreed.

16

Daniel and Sheila seemed happy to look after Emily for two or three days. When they'd heard that she was going to Dublin to sell her paintings, they were more than sympathetic; they knew she needed the money to get by. The swaying of the bus soon lulled her into a reverie that overprinted her awareness of the conductor and other passengers. She kept re-imagining Nick as he used to be: their first meeting in the Municipal Gallery and how relaxed he looked in his Aran sweater and cords. She had spotted him before he spotted her, and she stood admiring a late Corot, half-aware of a hovering somewhere in the emptiness behind her.

'They say he painted it on his deathbed.' She recognised the voice as English, but not posh English.

'Then there's hope for us all,' she said, turning to look at him.

'You mean we'll finally get there in extreme old age?'

Here, she thought, was an outgoing, straightforward man who'd never feel out of place at any time or in any country. It was her first impression of him, and how wrong it turned out to be. Most days found him sunk in the quicksands of the self, unmanned by a paralysis of the will brought on by too much self-questioning. Worst of all, he had no idea what made other people tick. In the rough-and-tumble world of indifferent men he was an unarmed innocent. His vulnerability was plain for all to see, and those who saw were not slow to take advantage. He himself was not unaware of his predicament. He once said that life was a naked run through a thorny wood in the dark.

On the fateful night of Paddy Canty's murder he came home in a state of shock. He could barely find the words to say he didn't do it. Naturally, she believed him. Now she was no longer certain. Why, if he was innocent, had he left her in the lurch? Would he seek out the anonymity of the city? He was probably holed up in Dublin, if not in London. Even in London he would probably avoid his usual haunts.

She went straight to the art shop and sold her paintings. The dealer could see that she was desperate. She parted with them for less than she would have liked. Afterwards she phoned Brendan Hurley and arranged to meet him in Neary's, a comfortable old pub that was not among Nick's favourite haunts. Over the first drink she told him her story. He listened with an occasional intake of breath. She could see that he felt uneasy. He kept looking around at the other drinkers, as if seeking an excuse to escape.

'How long has this been going on?' he asked.

'Two months or more.'

'Two months! You should have told me earlier. I had no idea.'

'No idea of what?'

'You may be sure the police are taking an interest in your every move. For all you know, they may have followed you here. They'll be keeping an eye on you, hoping you'll get in touch with Nick.'

'I don't care, I have nothing to hide. If I know Nick, he's in London by now.'

'I don't like it. Innocent or guilty, steer clear of the police has always been my policy.'

'Surely, you needn't worry.'

'Delma works in the Civil Service. She's very particular. I don't think we can go back to the flat. We'll go to a hotel instead. It's small and discreet. No questions asked.'

A surge of anger filled her breast. Telling herself that she would not have her evening ruined by his bossy sister, she finished her drink and said that she had an urgent call to make. When she finally got rid of him, she phoned Paul Flynn and asked if they could meet. It was the kind of thing she wouldn't have done a month ago. She felt used and put upon, and she blamed Nick for her wounded self-esteem.

Flynn was pleased to see her. He hugged her warmly and took her to one of her favourite restaurants. She enjoyed talking to him. She would have kept in touch with him if it hadn't been for Nick. While he would never suspect Brendan Hurley, he saw Flynn as the enemy of all married men, which amused her because they used to see quite a lot of him in the old days. It was Flynn who first told them that the American artist Rockwell Kent had spent a summer in the townland next to Leaca, and that he had made some of his best paintings there.

'You ought to see them,' he said. 'They're quite original. They really capture the otherworldly atmosphere of the place. It could be the making of you both.'

'What's his game?' Nick said afterwards.

'He must have gone off us. I think he's trying to get rid of us.' She wanted to make him see the absurdity of his suspicions, but it was no good.

'I know what it is. He has his eye on someone else's wife, and needs you out of the way for a while.'

Now, as she looked across the table at Paul, it occurred to her that there was something pathetic about Nick, though she hadn't seen it at the time. The restaurant menu was short, but she knew from experience that what it offered was good. She was hungry. She hadn't had a decent meal in ages. She chose whitebait to start with because it was filling, and for the main course she chose entrecôte pizzaiola. Paul couldn't have been hungry. She suspected that he might have already eaten. He had lobster bisque followed by grilled lemon sole with zucchini. Not a meal for a hearty eater, she told herself.

It was like old times. He amused her with the latest gossip. She told him about her painting and how she had come to Dublin to see her dealer. After her experience with Brendan Hurley, she felt reluctant to tell him about Nick.

'How is Nick? Still contemplating his *magnum opus*?' he asked finally.

'He may be contemplating his navel for all I know. He walked out on me two days ago and I haven't seen him since.'

She told him the whole story from start to finish. She couldn't stay in Leaca on her own now, she said. She would come back to Dublin as soon as she managed to sort something out. He sounded sympathetic. He invited her back to his flat for coffee. He told her that there was a spare bed and that he'd be delighted to put her up for the night. The flat consisted of a living room, bedroom, kitchen and bathroom. She washed her hair, and had a hot bath for the first time in six months. Cheekily, she put on his dressing gown, which she found hanging behind the bathroom door. He smiled and poured her a brandy. He put a record on the gramophone and sat beside her on the sofa. It was lovely being back in civilisation again. She felt as if someone was looking after her for a change.

He switched off the light, and they talked in the dark from their separate beds for a while.

'Time for beddy-byes,' he said finally, coming across to kiss her goodnight. Intuitively, she raised the covers and he slipped in beside her with an appreciative giggle. After the austerities of Leaca, she couldn't help feeling that there was something quite magical about it all.

'Will you ever get married?' she asked when they'd made love twice.

'Girls always ask me that.'

'You must admit it's unusual, being single at forty and so good in bed.'

'I'm happy as I am,' he said. 'I wouldn't change my life for love or money.'

He was an early riser. He cooked breakfast for them both and told her as he left for the office that she was welcome to come and stay whenever she fancied. She felt so grateful that she could have wept.

Sharon would be worried. She wouldn't know where to turn or what to do. Luckily, she had two or three paintings to sell. The money would keep her going till he'd managed to make Tom Barron see sense. Unfortunately, she wasn't the most practical of people. Ignorant of all domestic economy, she spent money like water while she had it, living entirely for the hour and the day, leaving him to worry about tomorrow and the day after.

Her vulnerability had brought them together. She had come out of a scorching love affair with a man she described as 'a brute in a three-piece suit'. She needed someone to look after her. She had turned to him because she considered him strong. He was drawn to her for different reasons, including her striking good looks. On that morning in the Municipal Gallery he couldn't take his eyes off her from the moment she walked in the door. She was tall and slender and she moved with an unhurried fluency of limb and body. He stood behind her, observing her absorption in the painting and the light on the tresses of her auburn hair. She talked about Corot and how his paintings fell into two distinct periods. When he saw her own paintings, he told himself that here was a woman who conveyed enough mystery to last any man a lifetime.

After four years together, he now knew what to expect. She was sensitive and impetuous. Their blazing rows would always be followed by frenetic, self-destructive sex. With her, sex was never far from the surface. He could see it in her paintings, which hinted at a life of ungovernable desire and urgent need. When they first came to Leaca, she began by painting portraits of the neighbours. She was taken with their strongly angular faces, bony noses and knurled hands. She had

a special gift for pastiche, choosing a style to suit each subject. For her portrait of Muiris, she chose vorticism. Muiris
took one look at the finished work and told her that she
should have painted the Gearrán instead. The following day
he pointed out the granite boulder he had in mind, which
gave her a new idea, though, of course, she did not share it
with anyone.

Over the next few months she set about painting rock
and cliff faces that bore a teasingly vague resemblance to
human features. Some of the paintings were quite arresting, and they weren't difficult to sell. From there she got the
idea of painting the lichen on rock faces close up. The lichen
formed imaginary tracery patterns, while the finished paintings hinted at an abstract design that refused to reveal its true
centre, and tantalised observers with the feeling that the key
to what they sought had been wilfully withheld. To him, it all
reeked of intellectual trickery rather than art, but he omitted
to enlighten her in the interest of domestic peace.

Next, she hit on the idea of making real landscape the
basis for abstract arrangements of colour and design. She had
Daniel translate the local place names into English for her, so
that she could use them as titles for her paintings. Thus the
Poll Caol became the Narrow Pool; the Poll Gorm, the Blue
Pool; and Poll Mhary, Mary's Pool.

Her dealer told her that one client whose opinion he
respected had described her paintings as 'fucking good', but
even that did not please her for long. She wanted art critics to
write about her, and the cognoscenti to talk about her at their
dinner parties. If only she could exhibit, even in a modest
way, everything else would follow, she said. At times he could
not help feeling a stab of envy. His stories weren't selling. But
for the pittance he made from working for the neighbours,
Sharon would be the only breadwinner in the house.

Curiously, their most stinging rows were not about money
but Emily. Sharon said that she was backward and did not say
much. When he insisted that Emily had no need to talk, that

she was happy playing with her doll, she said that he was confusing happiness with doziness. Luckily, whenever she went to Dublin, he had Emily all to himself for two days. In the summer she loved making daisy-chains and putting fairy thimbles on her fingers. In winter she would talk at length to Annie, her doll. As a baby, she was quiet. She slept a lot and rarely cried. Slow to learn reading, she would take a picture-book and pretend to read a story he had told her the previous day. She seemed to think that the story was in the pictures rather than the text, and nothing would convince her that she wasn't right. She was just ten months old when he first saw her. He fell in love with her immediately. He did not know who the father was. Sharon didn't say and he thought it best not to enquire.

Footsteps in the yard alerted him. Tom Barron entered with a mug of water and a slice of bread. He placed the mug on the floor and removed the gag with a grunt.

'I'm worried about Sharon, and I know she must be worried about me,' he said.

'You needn't worry about her. She's gone to Dublin to sell her paintings.'

'And what about Emily?'

'She's with Daniel and Sheila. She couldn't be in better hands.'

'Has no one reported me missing? Has no one organised a search for me?'

'The police are looking for you everywhere except here. They're keeping a watch on all the ports. You needn't worry. They won't find you as long as you stay with me.'

'That's what I want to talk to you about. How long are you going to hold me prisoner?'

'Until you tell the truth, however long it takes.'

'Well, you said it. I suppose you expect me to last forever without food and water.' His voice was thick. Croaking sounds rather than words emerged from his constricted throat.

'It isn't my choice. Whether you want to live or die is entirely up to you.'

He looked at Tom and realised from his stare that he was no longer the man he once knew.

'I'll make a concession. I'll have a cup of water,' he said. 'Just to show you I'm not as wrong-headed as you think.'

'It will make no difference. What I want from you is the truth.'

Tom held the mug to his lips and he drank slowly at first and then greedily.

'Water is sacred,' Tom said. 'There's neither life nor truth without it. Now will you tell me what really happened the night Paddy Canty was murdered?'

There was no hope of a settlement with Tom in his present mood. His mind was set on what he kept calling 'a true confession'. As he put the gag back on, Nick noticed the vacant look in his eyes. He was a changed man, no longer conscious of the consequences of his actions. To put it simply, his mind was not his own.

Alone once more, he counted the carbonised rafters for the umpteenth time. The whitewashed walls were stained by soot and what Tom called 'down rain' from the leaking roof. Less than a month ago he had helped Tom thatch the south side. Tom was friendly and chatty then. He'd told him that when his father built the present house, the old house had become the barn. Sometimes Tom referred to it as the barn, but more often than not he still called it 'the old house'. It had been a lovely day, the day of the thatching, and Nancy had cooked them a lovely meal. Now he realised that he did not appreciate it fully at the time. If only he could relive that day, he would no longer take it for granted.

He tried to stretch his legs, but no matter how he turned he felt uncomfortable. He was weak and cold and his legs and arms ached. His stomach threatened to cave in, leaving nothing behind except bone and empty skin. He closed his eyes, longing for the oblivion of sleep. He had lain awake for most of the night. Whenever he slept, he dreamed that he was being pursued by a tiger, and no matter how fast he ran, the tiger remained at his heels. Then as he was about to reach the house, the tiger leaped on his back and brought him down. He expected to be eaten, but the tiger merely licked his face. Its whiskers tickled his nostrils and his head was buried in its fur. The smell of cat's piss was suffocating. He woke shivering in a cold sweat. He did not know how long he could last out. Perhaps he should tell Tom Barron the truth.

Tom was once a decent and generous man. He had invited him out in his boat along with some of the others to fish lobsters several times, and he used to give him leftover crab claws to take home. The first time he went out was in June. As he left the house at half-past five, he thought he had never seen a morning so clear and calm. While they were hauling the last of the creels, Tom pointed to a white beach between the rocks where a fox was trotting along the drift-line, hoping to find a dead seabird washed ashore. He was a lovely fox with a long bushy tail that almost trailed the ground, and now and again he would pause to sniff at something just like a dog. He had the whole beach to himself, and they watched him as he trotted out of sight among the rocks.

'He's enjoying the peace and quiet,' Tom said. 'You'd know by his easy gimp that he isn't used to being disturbed.'

'He is monarch of all he surveys,' Cormac said.

'His right there is none to dispute,' Marcus Quinn agreed. They both had obviously learnt the same poem at school.

It was a magical moment that he would never forget. Feeling that he had been granted an incomparable insight into what it is to be a fox, he was so absorbed in the idea of 'foxness' that he resolved to write a story when he got home. He listened to his three companions as each told a story about their encounters with an animal that was more cunning and resourceful than any human being. In each story the fox was endowed with almost supernatural qualities, and when Cormac asked him if he had a fox story, he told them Aesop's fable about the fox that lost its tail.

'That isn't a true story.' Cormac shook his head.

'It's more like a parable,' Marcus said.

'A good story is a story you can tell again and again,' Cormac complained.

'That's right,' Marcus agreed. 'It doesn't teach a lesson. It's just a story and nothing else.'

He was left pondering this truth, if truth it was, for the rest of the day. He'd been out with Tom Barron in his boat many times since then, but he never saw the fox again. It was as if he had received a unique and unrepeatable revelation. It had been such a perfect morning, and perfect mornings were few. He would always remember the two pink clouds in the east, hanging motionless like torn curtains above the hills. All that seemed to have happened a billion years ago when the earth itself was young. On that morning he had given all his attention to the fox. If he had paid more attention to his neighbours, he might have written better stories. They lived on stories and for stories. Their whole conversation was made up of stories: stories about people alive and dead, about people they'd known and people their parents had known. The stories had been handed down. They had been moulded and polished by endless retelling, and time had given them an unquestionable authenticity.

The only story that seemed to have no established form was the story of Agent Cox's disappearance in the latter half of the last century. The local landlord shared his time between Belfast and London, rarely visiting his estate except for the salmon fishing. He left the running of his affairs to his agent Max Cox, who quickly got a name for cruelty, arrogance and greed. According to the local lore, his sudden disappearance in August 1863 occasioned a widespread search of the area that lasted into October. But in spite of the search, no body was ever found. Even Cox's horse had vanished without trace. Everyone seemed to have his own pet theory. Muiris said that he had gone for a swim because the day was hot and that he must have been eaten by a shark. Tom Barron was of the opinion that, suitably, he had drowned in the whirlpool at the base of Bud a' Diabhail. Cormac claimed that his death was an act of divine vengeance for having raped a young girl from Leaca and for having evicted her father for being in arrears with his rent. Marcus said that, more than likely, he had been taken by a mermaid who sympathised with the local girl he'd wronged.

What he could not understand was why everyone had a different story. He went to Belfast to check old copies of the *Belfast Telegraph* and discovered that local folklore was spectacularly inaccurate. Cox vanished in April 1881, not August 1863. His clothes were found on a lonely beach on the far side of the Tor Mór, and his horse was found shoeless with neither bridle nor saddle at the foot of Slieve League about twelve miles away. The only fact that folklore and the *Belfast Telegraph* agreed on was that his body had never been found.

The question that occurred to him now was whether the stories he'd been told were genuine folklore, or whether the people who told them were trying to mislead him. Perhaps the different versions of the story were meant to serve as a smokescreen to put outsiders off the scent. As a consequence of history, Leaca was an enclosed community. But why should they wish to mislead an outsider eighty years later? Surely he was being pathologically suspicious, imagining the worst. Daniel was the only man whose story was unlike all the others. He alone had said that Agent Cox had been murdered for his crime and his body buried deep in a bog.

He must have dozed off. He woke to hear a voice in the yard, Nancy calling, 'Chook, chook, chook,' to the hens. It was late afternoon. She was giving them the potatoes left over from dinner mixed with a handful of oatmeal. What would he not give for tea, boiled eggs, soda bread, and butter? To get them he would have to throw in the towel. He could last over a week without food. Tom was bound to get rattled before then. When he reached that point, he would gladly believe any story that would get him off the hook. But why wait till then? What if he should encourage him to get rattled by pretending to be dying? Tomorrow morning he would demand to see the priest and ask for what they called extreme unction.

17

*T*here was no sound in the kitchen, apart from the whispering of the rain outside and the clacking of Nancy's knitting needles. She was sitting in the chimney corner, turning the heel of a sock, while Tom was seated by the window, reading yesterday's *Irish News*, which Daniel had given him earlier in the day.

'Listen to this,' he said. 'Northern Ireland police have been alerted in case Ambrose should try to cross the border in order to escape to Scotland or England. All ports in the Republic are already under surveillance.'

'That must please you.' Nancy scratched her head with the point of a knitting needle.

'Why should it please me?'

'Because no one has thought of looking here in Leaca.'

'When the police get a bee in their bonnets, they can think of nothing but the bee.'

'Isn't that you down to the ground now? You think Ambrose is guilty, and nothing else matters. Where will it end? That's what I'd like to know.'

'It will end when he tells me the truth.'

'I think you're mad, Tom. The poor boy is out there in the barn in this cold weather. He can't live on water alone for much longer.'

'You can live on water for a fortnight. Remember the sailor who came ashore during the war? He had a barrel of water and nothing else.'

'That was in the height of summer. He was on a raft, and he had the best of chocolate. I had some of it myself, and so did you. It was very good chocolate.'

'Well, I'll offer Ambrose some chocolate and we'll see if he's tempted to eat it.'

'Ambrose is every bit as stubborn as you. If he's innocent, he won't give in.'

'All right, we'll put him to the test. Give me a bar of chocolate and I'll take it out to him.'

'Where would I get chocolate? You're only saying it to annoy me…. But maybe you'll listen to Jim. I wrote to him yesterday and asked him to come home.'

'Why did you go and do a thing like that now?'

'He said he'd come home to give you a hand with the turf-cutting, remember?'

'That isn't why you wrote to him.'

'While he's here, maybe he'll talk to you about that young boy out there.'

'You shouldn't have done it, Nancy. I have enough on my mind as it is.'

'I'll put on the kettle and make the tea now. You could offer some to Ambrose. It might warm him up, and it might show him you're not a savage, but a human being.'

He put down the paper and watched as she filled the kettle from the water bucket. He put on his cap and took the mug of hot tea from her. It was still raining heavily as he crossed the yard. Ambrose, who was lying with his back to the door, moaned as he approached.

'Here, I've brought you some hot tea instead of cold water. It will warm you up.'

Ambrose moaned again as he removed the gag. His eyes were closed and he looked pale and pinched.

'Here, drink this.'

'I don't want tea. I want to see a priest.'

'What can the priest do for you? You're not a Catholic, are you?'

'There's no vicar in the parish. A Catholic priest is the next best thing.'

'You can confess to me, if it's confession that's on your mind.'

'I feel terrible. I'm dying, can't you see?! I want the last rites. Only a priest can give me those.'

'You're very religious all of a sudden. Maybe you'd like to go to Mass on Sunday as well.'

'Can't you see I'm dying?' He grimaced and moaned again.

'How do you know you're dying?'

'When your turn comes, you'll know as well. And I hope you won't need to convince anyone, because you won't have the energy to do it.' He turned away and closed his eyes.

He was afraid to put the gag back on. He closed the door and bolted it. He was badly shaken, worried in case Ambrose might be telling the truth for a change. He really didn't know what to do.

'Well, did he drink the tea?' Nancy asked.

'No, he wants to see the priest. He's pretending to be dying but he doesn't fool me.'

'Have you lost your wits, Tom? He probably is dying, and I won't allow you to have it on your conscience. It's freezing cold out there. We'll take him into the house and put him in Jim's room. He'll have a proper bed, and we'll kill the black hen that isn't laying.'

'You'll kill Ambrose if you give him too much to eat all at once. The doctor would only allow the sailor thin gruel and milk for three whole days.'

'We'll give him the soup, then. I'll make it good and thick. We'll have to look after him till he gets strong again.'

'This is crazy, Nancy. It doesn't make any sense.'

'It makes sense to me. Go out now and bring him in. I'll put a fire in Jim's room and make it comfortable and warm.'

Reluctantly, he admitted to himself that she was right. It would be terrible if anything should happen to him. He would never be able to disagree with her again.

He was shivering when Tom brought him in. Tom undid the shackles and they put him to bed straight away. She gave him hot milk to drink and afterwards a little gruel on a spoon. Curiously, he wasn't ravenous. At first he seemed reluctant to eat anything. It was like feeding a baby. She had to force the spoon between his teeth. She lit a fire in Jim's bedroom and got Tom to kill the black hen and hang her up in the hen-house to let the blood drain away. She would pluck and clean her and cook her for tomorrow's dinner. It was best not to give him too much to eat all at once.

She sat knitting by the bedside in order to keep an eye on him and in case he needed anything. At first Tom was worried that he was only pretending, but he had come to accept that he was seriously ill. He was sleeping now, facing the wall with his back to her. She could hear his breathing which was the breathing of someone who was feverish. She leant over the bed and felt his forehead. As she had expected, it was moist and hot. He had a temperature. She would have to look in on him from time to time during the night.

He was muttering something to himself, she couldn't make out what. It was something about a tiger. He was obviously raving. He wasn't making much sense, poor boy. She put aside her knitting and said two decades of the rosary to herself. Coming up to bedtime, he opened his eyes and looked round him in alarm. He tried to raise himself in the bed but he fell back helplessly again.

'Where am I?' he asked hoarsely.

'You're in Jim's room. Don't worry now, you'll be all right in a day or two.'

'I want to talk to Sharon. She must be worried stiff.'

'You can't talk to her yet. It's too dangerous. The guards are looking for you everywhere, I'm afraid.'

'But I can't stay here.'

'You'll have to stay till you get your strength back. Would you like me to make you another hot drink?'

'Yes, that would be good.'

'And I'll make you a nice bowl of stirabout as well. If you need anything else, just let me know.'

When she went back to the kitchen, she found Tom reading *Old Moore* with the smoky oil lamp at his elbow. His steel-rimmed spectacles were tight against the bridge of his nose. They made him look like Pope Pius himself. At times he behaved like a pope, but she knew better than to agree with everything he said. It was just as well that she had the sense to stand up to him, because he'd get into big trouble if left to do everything his own way.

'He's awake at last,' she said.

'I'll go in and talk to him. Make him see sense.'

'No, you won't. You'll only frighten him. We need to look after him till he's well again.'

'Did he say anything?'

'He asked for Sharon but I told him he couldn't see her yet.'

'What if he tries to escape?'

'He's too weak to escape. In his present state he wouldn't get from here to the door.'

He had surfaced from suffocating darkness, from the bottom of a slimy well. No one had come to help him. He had climbed up painfully, from one slippery foothold to the next. At first he thought he wouldn't make it. If he had lost faith in himself for a single moment and slipped back down, he would have ended up in the coils of the python at the bottom. And from the python there was no escape.

Compared with the mattress in the barn, the bed was warm and soft. She had lit a fire. He could smell the turf smoke from where he lay. They'd obviously been worried in case he wouldn't pull through. To tell the truth, he felt terrible, and it had come on so suddenly. He hadn't realised how weak he was till he tried to get out of bed. He would have to take things easy, bide his time till his strength returned.

On the way up towards the light he'd had visions, visions of the past, the same nagging images over and over again. His coldly indifferent stepfather, his snobbish Aunt Betty, Hugh Gardiner, the preposterous manager of the advertising firm he worked for in Berkeley Square.

'Good morning, Ambrose. Have you used Pear's soap? Lovely day for a Guinness. Nothing like a good slogan, eh. Look sharp, feel sharp. Look sharp, think sharp: that's my philosophy, Ambrose. I think up my best slogans in the bath.' Gardiner was a self-infatuated twit. He saw everyone else as a passenger who would never pay his way.

Nancy came in with a mug of hot milk. Slowly, he pulled himself up in the bed and she put the pillows to his back for support.

'You'll feel better after you've drunk this. I'll make soup for you tomorrow. We killed a hen that wasn't laying. She never laid an egg all year.'

'Chicken soup! I wouldn't mind a drumstick as well. And the wishbone. Don't forget to keep the wishbone for me, will you?'

'You mustn't eat too much all at once. A little at a time till you get your strength back. You're feeling better already, I can tell.'

He thought it best not to appear too perky. He put down the mug and closed his eyes.

'The milk will make you heavy. You'll sleep now.'

He sank down in the bed and turned to the wall. She put her hand on his forehead but he did not open his eyes. When he woke, he was alone. The fire had died down in the grate, and the little red oil lamp was burning on the mantelpiece. It was almost three in the morning. He hauled himself up in the bed and swung his legs out over the side. When he tried to stand up, he felt dizzy. He gripped the bedstead, and kneeling down, drew the enamel po out from under the bed. The effort of stooping made him sweat. He went down on his knees and held the po with both hands as he urinated into it. The yellow water came in a slow trickle. It was so strong-smelling that it made his nostrils twitch. He breathed a sigh of relief when the trickle finally stopped.

He lay on his back and tried not to think, because thinking kept him awake. It would take him at least a week to recover his strength. By then Sharon would have given up all hope. She would go back to Dublin because there she could count on friends. She needed regular release from her inner demons; she wouldn't last long without a man. The obvious candidate was Flynn. He was a man for all women. Sixty or sixteen, he made no academic distinctions. He had made a pass at her more than once before. Sharon was the kind of woman who invited passes. She was chatty and carefree. At least that was the impression she liked to give. Once you got to know her, she was a congeries of contradictions. On her own she was given to brooding. She mulled over every inconsequential comment, imagining slights where none was intended. She was not the easiest of women. Still, he couldn't conceive of life without her. They'd been together for four years now, and for most of the time they were happy. They fought like weasels and made love like tigers. Well, perhaps not quite like tigers. He'd read somewhere that tigers can mate over a hundred times in two days while the female is receptive. Tigers didn't spend too much time over it, though. Twenty seconds flat, whereas Sharon was a skilled practitioner of procrastination, who expected an equal degree of stamina from her man. She could last all night, and then she'd fall asleep utterly exhausted. She'd be talking to him one minute and snoring in his ear the next.

She was a lively conversationalist. They talked about everything that came to mind, everything except Flynn. She'd known him before they met. He'd seen them kissing at a party, and for all he knew it hadn't stopped there. In the early days he used to keep an eye on Flynn, just in case. One night he was standing under a tree in the park opposite the house where she lived, waiting to see if Flynn would appear. After a while he realised that a man was lurking in the shadows about twenty yards to the left. He was tall and thin with a flat cap. For a moment he imagined he was seeing his own ghost. The dark, brooding figure stood for over an hour inside the railings of the park, gazing up at the lighted window on the second floor. He himself stood looking at the man's back until finally, as the headlights of a passing car caught his profile, he knew the man was Flynn. How could he have been so stupid? Going across to the no-longer-mysterious figure, he asked him for a light, though he knew Flynn didn't smoke. He looked put out. The great Casanova caught gazing at a woman's window like a lovesick schoolboy. He never told Sharon. How could he? The things that vexed and haunted him would only diminish him in her eyes if she knew. Certain things troubled him deeply. His suspicion that Flynn was Emily's natural father was one of these.

When they moved to Leaca, he got partial relief from the demon. Flynn was no longer on his mind twenty-four hours a day, but he would break the even flow of his thoughts whenever Sharon went to Dublin. On her return he would ask her if she'd met him and invariably she'd say she hadn't. That would not satisfy him, however. For weeks his mind would return to Flynn whenever he was alone, fishing from a rock, sitting on a cliff top, or walking on the hill behind the house. At times there was no escaping the demon, and now he had returned with a vengeance. Somehow or other he would have to make his way to Dublin, because wherever Flynn was, there he would find Sharon.

In the early days he had tried to avoid Flynn, seeing him as one of those frauds who boned up on art in order to flatter women artists. In moments of extreme self-doubt he saw him as an implacable enemy. Now he knew better. Flynn was his inchoate self, and as such a fitting subject for investigation. He must be pursued, questioned, and pinned down as a lepidopterist might pin a white or red admiral to a piece of cardboard. After all, it was possible that Mr Hyde knew things and had things to say that only Dr Jekyll could construe.

What he could not understand was the nature of her relationship with Flynn. In a perfect world perhaps she would have chosen him, or perhaps she realised that he was not a man who could sustain a one-to-one relationship for long. His appetite was for novelty and variety. As Brendan Hurley put it, he gave as much thought to a change of women as other men give to a change of socks. Sharon had an instinctive understanding of these things. She would never be content to be seen as one among many. She must always be the one and only. As she said one morning over breakfast, 'I'm the only artist in Leaca. It's a small thing, I suppose, but it's something.'

The only artist in Leaca. It set her apart from everyone else. She didn't talk to people because there was no point. They wouldn't understand her anyway, she said. In spite of that, he wouldn't have described her as stuck up. She just wasn't interested in other people. At least not in the way he himself was. She could tell him who had an interesting face, but she had no interest in the mind or experience that had made it so. She found the neighbours' stories tedious whereas he found in them a reflection of a world he sensed all around him but could only discern vaguely in the blur of half-light. He was the man who hung back on the edge of the crowd, an observer rather than a participant. Sharon was neither. She did not observe and she refused to participate. She closed her eyes and invented a world of her own.

'Tell me, What's wrong with me?' she once demanded in the blistering heat of a post-coital argument.

'You've got the wrong mind in the right body,' he said, to be awkward.

'And you've got the right mind in the wrong body. That's why you're a writer; it's your snivelling way of getting even with the world. If you could fill my eye as a man, you'd never write another word. I'm your only Muse. You need me for your art more than I need you for mine.' They were the most hurtful words he'd ever had from her. She could be a right bitch at times.

One Sunday last September he took her to Daniel's to listen to the All Ireland Football Final, which was being played for the first time in the Polo Grounds, New York. Daniel owned the only wireless in Leaca, and all the men of Leaca had gathered to listen. Muiris was there with his good ear close to the set, and so were Paddy Canty, Tom Barron, Cormac, Marcus, Neil Durkin and Red Miller. Sharon and Sheila, the only two women, sat on opposite sides of the fire while the men gathered round the table as if proximity to the source of the sound would bring them closer to the scene of the action. Cavan was playing Kerry, and Kerry was red-hot favourite. Michael O'Hehir was giving the commentary, and what an impassioned commentary it turned out to be. It was the most exciting match he'd ever heard broadcast. Kerry soon built up an eight-point lead, but two of their goals were disallowed and frees given instead. Muiris was rooting for Kerry, while everyone else was shouting for Cavan. In the second half the tide turned, and Cavan forged ahead. Muiris lost his cool. He would whack his stick against his boot every time Mick Higgins, Tony Tighe or some other Cavan player got the ball. It went to extra time, and Michael O'Hehir had to plead with the powers above to allow the programme to overrun. It was the greatest match ever. When the final whistle blew on a Cavan victory, Muiris got to his feet and declared that Kerry had been robbed.

'Give us a fair referee, and we'll play you again,' he had said, storming out of the kitchen.

There was general hilarity at his departure. The post mortem that followed lasted longer than the game itself. Cormac said that if Kerry had travelled to New York by air, they would have won. It was the sea journey, not the referee, that banjaxed them. As usual, Marcus agreed with Cormac. He said that Cavan had got over the plane journey in two days and had a whole week to train in New York while Kerry were being sick on the high seas.

Sharon said on the way home that they'd all lost what-ever common sense they were born with. She said it was her first Gaelic football match and her last. Yet the following day she drew a sketch of the gathering with the wireless in the centre of the table surrounded by faces that pressed against each other and against the set. The faces were distorted with unspoken passion and the ears closest to the set seemed bigger than the ear on the other side of each head.

'It's a winner,' he told her. 'You should take it further. You mustn't leave it there.'

She spent a week working on it, almost non-stop. She called the finished oil painting simply 'Football', and curiously all the heads that crowded into the square canvas seemed to have taken on the shape of a ball.

'It isn't the game we listened to,' he said. 'It's every Gaelic football match ever broadcast.'

That was Sharon. She wasn't a recorder of the particular. She was a maker. Yet her painting lacked the stamp of true originality. It reminded him of a mural by Diego Rivera, so crowded with faces that it threatened to burst its frame. Sharon would never become a great artist because her gaze wasn't steady enough to meet the truth that looked her in the eye. He did not blame himself for omitting to tell her so. Instead he blamed her for being the kind of artist who could not bear to hear it.

Among her saving graces was her wicked sense of humour. She simply couldn't get over the business of Red Miller's lamb, a white-faced ewe lamb that Miller gave to his wife as a peace offering after a row. Madge kept her lamb in the field below the house, a fenced field that was proof against her husband's ram, and she watched her pet grow into a lovely ewe. When the ewe was eighteen months old, she gave birth to a ram lamb in the month of September, which caused a stir among the neighbours. It was known for ewes to lamb as late as July but no one had ever heard of a ewe giving birth in September. Red Miller had withdrawn his ram from his out-grazed flock the previous December, and anyway there was no sign that a ram had broken through the fenced field where the pet ewe had been grazing. For a week or more the ewe and her lamb were at the centre of all discussion in Leaca. Cormac said that only the ewe knew the answer and that she was making no comment. Daniel said that it was a case of virgin birth, that it proved beyond doubt that parthenogenesis was not a fiction. Muiris was more down to earth. He took one look at the ram lamb and declared that he was the spitting image of Red Miller himself. When Sharon heard about Muiris's comment, she was beside herself with glee. She drew a sketch of a lamb with a big fleshy nose that bore a remarkable resemblance to Red Miller's. On seeing the sketch, Muiris gave one of the silent laughs for which he was famous. His jaw trembled soundlessly, and he told her that on no account must she show it to Red Miller. After that Muiris could do no wrong in Sharon's eyes. She used to say that he was the only man in Leaca who shared her sense of humour and appreciated the nature of her artistic gift.

Thinking about Sharon was not conducive to sleep. He lay on his back with his arms by his side and deliberately recalled the tranquillity of the day he'd had his first sight of Leaca. They'd arrived in the lower glen on a June afternoon and followed the road as it climbed between bare hills of rock, scree and heather. The road entered a pass between two mountains and curled in a wide loop to run along the shore of a narrow lough. He was giving his whole attention to the placid water, when suddenly they came upon a little hamlet overlooking a stony beach. Beyond the beach lay the sea, and beyond the sea lay Newfoundland.

'This is *our* new-found land,' he said to Sharon. 'Here we'll find peace. It's a little haven, if not a little heaven.'

'It's wild and beautiful,' she said. 'But is there anything to eat apart from heather and rushes?'

He must have dropped off. Nancy woke him with a cup of tea at eight.

'Did you sleep?' she asked.

'Off and on. I feel very weak.' He thought it best to let her know that he was still far from well.

'You're looking better. Much better. I'll bring you your stirabout in a minute. We'll be having chicken for supper. It will be a welcome change from salt fish. It gives me terrible heartburn, so it does.'

It was good porridge, neither too thin nor too thick, and he ate it slowly with milk and sugar. Already he could feel his strength returning. Soon he would be able to escape.

18

*W*hen Jim Barron got his mother's letter, he had to read between the lines. She didn't say why she wanted to see him, but he could tell that it wasn't just the turf-cutting that was bothering her.

'Daddy is unhappy,' she wrote. 'He isn't himself these days. He has too many things on his mind.' He had never known his father to be weighed down by life's burdens. He was a solid, no-nonsense man who devoted himself entirely to farming and fishing. Perhaps he was worried about his health, but that was unlikely. He never suffered from anything more serious than an occasional bout of sciatica and now and again the common cold.

He always enjoyed his trips home. Leaca was one of the few places on God's earth that never seemed to change, because any change that did occur was too gradual to be perceptible. Old people died, of course, but life went on as before. The only evidence of the twentieth century was Daniel's car and wireless.

Paddy Canty had died since he was home last. It was a shocking business. Even now he found it difficult to believe that such a thing could have happened in Leaca. Paddy occupied a special position in the local folklore. When he was a young man, a neighbour who was too ill to go to Ardara fair asked him to go in his place and sell a springer cow on his behalf. Paddy sold the heifer and gratefully pocketed the money. He had never been in possession of such a tidy sum before. He walked to Derry and took the first boat to America.

Six months later he sent double the price of the heifer to his neighbour, and from then on he sent him three dollars every Christmas as further interest. When the neighbour was on his deathbed, he said that the heifer had been the making of him.

'If I had days to live,' he added, 'I'd die a dollar million-aire.' From then on, Paddy was seen as a man who could do no wrong. He was as honest as St Patrick and as steady as St Peter himself.

Jim was fond of Paddy. He had begun compiling a book of his stories and sayings. Now he would have to cast his net wider and make it into a book about the vanishing life of Leaca. He would call it *Mountain Men*. It would be a record of the life and culture of a dying community—dying because once this generation of farmers and fishermen had gone, there would be no one left to take their place. He should have come home to Paddy's wake and funeral but he had been delving into a scandal involving a cabinet minister at the time, and his editor advised him not to take his eye off the ball. A journalist's life was like that. Always up against time, tide, and editors whose appetite for stories about sexual irregularity knew no bounds. Now he had taken a whole week off as part of his annual holiday. He would spend the days with his father on the bog. After a sedentary winter the exercise would do him good. He was looking forward to talking to the neigh-bours again, particularly Muiris who was now the oldest man in Leaca. He wasn't as easygoing as Paddy. He was proud and touchy and given to bragging, but he knew how to tell a story and he had some interesting stories to tell.

He arrived home in the afternoon while his father was on the hill tending the lambs. His mother came out to wel-come him when she heard the car. She took him into the old house and told him about the 'lodger' in his room. It was a long story. She was quite breathless by the time she'd finished.

She grasped his hand and said, 'I'm pleased you've come home. You must talk to Daddy. He won't listen to me. Try to make him see sense.'

He didn't know what to think. His first thought was that here were the guts of a good story, but how could he use it without getting his parents into trouble? They obviously didn't see eye to eye about what to do, and the last thing he wanted was to act as referee. He probably felt closer to his mother than his father. She wrote regularly and kept him primed with all the local news. On the other hand, he didn't want to fall out with his father, whom he'd always admired for his practical commonsense. He was a man who could turn his hand to whatever needed to be done, and if he didn't have the right tool for the job, he'd be sure to find a makeshift substitute. Clearly, he would have to tread carefully. What they both wanted was a way out of the impasse. A walk on the hill might help clear his mind.

When he'd had a cup of tea with his mother, he changed into his old clothes and found an old pair of wellingtons that his father had discarded. As the wellingtons were a size too big, his mother gave him a pair of thick woollen socks, which he put on over his own. He drew on his old duffle coat, and his mother told him that all he needed now was a string of tin cans to pass for a tinker.

At the end of the lane he met Muiris returning from the hill. He was carrying his shepherd's crook and wearing his Antarctic hat. He stood facing the low sun, squinting as he tried to look like Shackleton.

'You're home for a few days,' he said.

'Just for the turf-cutting.'

'Do you think you're up to it? The *sleán* is heavier than the pen, I'll bet.'

'And healthier, too. Nothing beats working in the open on a good day.'

'What's the latest news on Ambrose?' From the way Muiris changed the subject, he wondered if this were a trick question.

'The last I heard they were still looking for him.'

'They'll never find him,' Muiris said.

171

'You think he's already slipped through the net?'

'If I know anything, he's beyond the Jordan by now.'

'The guards have alerted the English police. If he's in England, he could be arrested and sent back.'

'But he may not be in England. Have you thought of that?'

'You mean he may have gone further? I suppose he could be on a boat to Canada or Australia. But he wouldn't necessarily be safe on a boat. Dr Crippen was arrested on a ship bound for Quebec.'

'Poison was Crippen's weapon. A length of cod-line was Ambrose's. If they catch him, I'll write to the hangman and tell him to use cod-line.' Muiris whacked the ferrule of his crook against his boot.

'I'll call down to see you one evening,' Jim said.

'And we'll swap stories over a glass or two. I can tell you some good ones about Ambrose. I'd better be going before the quare one catches up with us.'

Sharon was coming from the well with a bucket of water. Jim sat on the ditch and waited till she came up. She was wearing a white smock with a blue apron over it, and her hair was swept up in an untidy bun at the back.

'Let me carry the bucket for you. I'm doing nothing else.'

She smiled and put down the bucket with a little sigh. As they walked up the road, she asked him if he'd heard any news of Nick.

'Only what you've heard. The police think he'd already left the country by the time he was reported missing.'

'I doubt that somehow. He didn't have any money, you see.'

'He could have got a lift to Dublin and borrowed money from a friend.'

'I know his friends. They're all skint like himself.'

'The whole thing is a great mystery from start to finish,' he said.

When they reached the house, she invited him in for a cup of tea. 'It will be black tea,' she added. 'I don't have any milk, I'm afraid.'

The kitchen was in a state of confusion, everything scattered higgledy-piggledy, nothing in its proper place. The little girl was sitting on the hearth, putting her doll to sleep in a shoebox. The fire had died down, and there was no turf in the basket in the chimney corner.

'Let me bring in some turf,' he said.

'We're running low. There's only enough left for tomorrow.'

He brought in an armful of turf and a few sticks and got the fire going again. She hung the kettle on the pothook over the fire and sat down beside him on what used to be a settle-bed.

'Help me,' she said. 'You're a journalist; you're trained to see things from every point of view.' His left hand was resting on his knee, and she took it and pressed it between both her own.

'How can I help you?' he asked seriously.

'You can make people realise there's more than one possibility. Nick has been branded a criminal without trial. Surely that can't be right.'

'The police think he absconded to escape justice. I can't change their minds.'

'You can write an article from a different angle. It's only good journalism to question what everyone else thinks is gospel. Isn't that what journalists do?'

'But it needs to have the ring of truth even though it may not be true.'

'Look at me, Jim. Do you think I'm lying?'

'No, I don't think you're lying. Like the rest of us, you're totally in the dark.'

'I know Nick. He would never have left Emily and me in the lurch like this. Something must have happened to him, something he hadn't foreseen.'

'According to the reports I've read, you said you woke up to find him missing from the bed. He must have had a reason to get up so early.'

'He used to walk on the cliffs whenever he couldn't sleep. He was fond of the sea. He could have fallen down a bank.'

'Did you tell that to the police?'

'The police think he's a murderer, and so does everyone else here. That's the problem. He's been found guilty *in absentia*. Isn't that how you journalists put it?'

'Not on my paper. You must be thinking of *The Irish Times*.'

'Anyway, there's nothing I can do because no one will listen to me. You could help me if you had a mind to. You could write an article putting out my point of view. You don't have to say it's my view. You can give it what you call "the ring of truth".'

He thought for a moment.

'I'm on holiday, he said, 'but I'll see what I can do.'

'You could get another journalist to write it. You could tell him everything I said.'

He looked at her and realised with a sense of helplessness that he wanted to go to bed with her. In spite of the tousled hair, she was a very attractive woman, more attractive than a layabout like Ambrose deserved.

'I must be going now,' he said.

'You won't wait for a cup of tea?'

'I'd better be going. I'll bring you some milk and a creel of turf tomorrow. I'm sure the little one likes milk in her tea.'

'And you'll remember what I said?' She took his hand again and looked at him with imploring eyes.

'My editor's a bastard. What gets published is not up to me.'

'I know about writing because of Nick,' she said. 'A writer can make anything sound true. I know about painting as well. Let me show you something before you go.'

She went to the bedroom and came back with a painting, which she stood on the table against the wall. It showed a tall, thin man and his sheepdog against a bleached-out landscape. The man was leaning on his staff, looking left, and the dog by his side was facing right. Behind the two stark figures was the outline of a mountain he recognised as Sliabh Tuaidh. The man's scrutinising glance suggested a forceful and wily mind, and his self-conscious pose challenged all who would seek to probe behind the mask. It was a painting of hidden psychological power, he thought.

'It's obviously meant to be Muiris and his dog.'

'Is it, now?' she smiled.

'Well, it reminds me of Muiris but I know it isn't Muiris. If it were just Muiris, it would have less force. It isn't what it tells you but the questions it makes you ask.'

'You see what I mean? Now you know how to write your article.'

She didn't give up easily. He reckoned she might be an interesting woman to get to know.

'I'll do my best,' he said. 'But what will you do if he doesn't come back?'

She looked at him searchingly for a moment. 'I can't stay here on my own forever,' she replied.

19

On his return he found his father and mother lighting a fire in the kitchen of the old house. Having made a shakedown in the corner, complete with sheets and blankets, they had cleared a space on the floor around the bed and placed a kitchen chair on each side of the fireplace.

'So this is my room for the night!' Jim smiled. 'You're certainly making sure I'll be comfortable.'

'No, you'll be in your own room. This is for Ambrose,' his mother said.

'If he's still feeling poorly, let him stay where he is and I'll sleep out here.'

'That would never do. I've spoken to him. He's feeling much better. He says he doesn't mind.'

'He probably thinks he can escape,' his father said.

'He must know there's no point with the police on his tail.'

'Somehow I don't think that would deter him.'

'I'll go and get your tea.' His mother went off with her hands in her apron pockets.

His father sat on one of the chairs and reached out his hands towards the fire as if to warm the palms. Hunched over the hearth, he looked serious and preoccupied. He had got himself into a mess. Jim didn't like to see him look so defeated.

'What did your mother tell you about Ambrose?'

'She said he was at death's door for a day or two.'

'Women exaggerate. It wasn't that bad.'

'It still isn't good. You know you can't keep him here forever.'

'He's a headstrong devil. I wanted him to sign a confession but he wouldn't. You're an educated man, Jim. Your word carries more weight than mine. Maybe he'll listen to you.'

'A confession signed under duress is a non-starter. It isn't worth the paper it's written on.'

'So what must we do?'

'The simple thing is to let the police deal with him. They seem to have the evidence now. Once they get hold of him, they'll charge him.'

'But isn't that the problem! They don't have any new evidence. I was talking to McNally yesterday. They think he ran away to escape justice. That's the only reason they want to interview him.'

'It's absurd.'

'Well, that's how it is. If I hand him over now, I'll be in trouble with the law for wrongful imprisonment, can't you see? I could even be charged with perverting the course of justice, as they say. Besides, if the neighbours get wind of his whereabouts, his life won't be worth a fart. It's back to Agent Cox and the Triangle again.'

'The Triangle? Surely not. Not in this day and age.'

'If you don't believe me, ask Daniel. Like me, he would have nothing to do with it.'

'Would Ambrose agree to vanish in return for a sum of money?' Jim wondered.

'Where would I get enough money? Besides, I'm sure he wouldn't go anywhere without Sharon and the wee one.'

They were seated on opposite sides of the fire, looking at the flames beginning to take hold. For a long time neither spoke.

'I suppose I've been lucky in life,' his father said. 'I've never been in a pickle like this before.'

'There must be a way out. Ambrose sees himself as a writer. I think I know a trick that might tickle his vanity. I'll talk to him this evening. Who knows, he may discover where his true interest lies.'

When they'd eaten, he went into the bedroom to see Ambrose, who was sitting up reading about himself in an old copy of the *Irish News*. He looked gaunt and pale, barely recognisable with his black stubble. Jim couldn't help noticing his dainty hands. They could easily have been the hands of a priest. He found it difficult to believe that they belonged to the man who had garrotted Paddy Canty.

'How are you feeling?' he asked.

'A bit stronger than yesterday. Your mother is as good as any nurse.'

'I think it's time you and I had a talk. My father held you because he caught you trying to break into the house. He's convinced it was you who murdered Paddy Canty, and so are all the neighbours. I don't mind telling you that if any of the neighbours got to know where you are, your life wouldn't be worth the steam off your piss. The police are also on your tail, so I wouldn't advise you to try to escape.'

'I know the police are after me, but I refuse to believe my life's in danger from my neighbours.'

'You heard of Max Cox, the landlord's agent.'

'The man who disappeared and was never found?'

'He didn't just disappear. He was murdered and buried on the mountain. Everyone who was ever born in Leaca could show you where.'

Jim told him about the Triangle and how the idea had been resurrected as a means of getting justice for Paddy Canty. Ambrose put aside the newspaper and for a long time just stared vacuously at the foot of the bed.

'I'd like you to know I didn't do it,' he said. 'You must believe me. I need your help.'

'I don't see how I can help you.'

'I'll tell you everything I know about that terrible night. We were down to our last shilling and Sharon didn't have any finished paintings to sell. I knew that Paddy Canty had sold his wethers at Ardara fair and that he was bound to have money in the house. I got up in the small hours unbeknown to Sharon and went over to Paddy's to see if I could rob him. People used to say he was the richest man in Leaca. The way I saw things he mightn't miss a pound or two. Well, when I got to his house, the back door was open. I waited a long time because I didn't know what to think. Finally, I entered and shone my torch. He was sitting in his armchair with his head resting on his chest. I'll never forget it. I knew right away that he was dead. I didn't touch anything and I didn't steal anything. I just made for home as fast as I could. You must believe me. It's my only hope.'

'Did you realise then that he'd been murdered?'

'I didn't spot the marks on his neck but I knew from the terrible expression on his face. He looked as if he was trying to scream and couldn't. It's a sight I'll never forget.'

'Did you tell that to the police?'

'No, I couldn't admit I was there at the scene of the crime. They would have taken it as an admission of guilt.'

'It would have been better than telling a lie.'

'It's too late to change my story now.'

'If what you say is true, someone else must have murdered Paddy Canty.'

'And it's in that person's interest to pin the rap on me.'

He looked into Ambrose's sunken eyes and then at his hands. He had no convincing reason to believe him. For all he knew he might be spinning another yarn. Yet he sensed that he was talking to a man who was telling the truth out of sheer desperation, not because he wanted to but because it was the only thing left for him to do.

'I need time and opportunity to clear my name. That's where you can help me. I'm relying on you to get me out of here. I won't be a free man till the real culprit is caught.'

'He won't be caught while the police believe you're the murderer. They've stopped looking for anyone else. You'll have to tell them the story you just told me. They may believe you or they may not. It's a risk you'll have to take.'

'Well, it's a risk I'm not willing to take. I've got friends in Dublin. If you could get me there, I'd lie low till I manage to clear my name.'

'Where would you live in Dublin?'

'I don't know yet.'

'And what would you live on?'

'I'm a writer. You might be able to push freelance work in my direction till I find my feet.'

'You've worked everything out.'

'I've been thinking about it ever since your mother said you were coming home.'

'Well, let me put an idea to you. You've had, shall we say, an interesting experience. Handled in the right way, it would make a good story. You could fill me in on the details and I would write it.'

'I don't need a ghost writer. I'm well able to write it myself.'

'You could write it, but will it sell? That's the question.'

'I'll write it and you can edit it, but I must have the final say.'

'And my paper must have exclusive publication rights.'

'You haven't left me much choice.'

'I'll be going back to Dublin at the weekend and I'll take you with me. In the meantime you can start writing, and if you're sensible you won't shave. If we're stopped by the police, I'll say you were thumbing a lift and I picked you up on the road. Is that clear?'

'What about Sharon and Emily? I can't leave them here.'

'I'll see what I can do. I'm sure something can be arranged.'

When Jim told his father about his conversation with Ambrose, he shook his head. 'What if you get into trouble with the police?' he asked.

'Do you have a better idea?'

'How can you be so sure he's innocent?'

'I'm not absolutely sure but I'm almost sure. I'm convinced he isn't play-acting.'

For a moment neither of them said anything.

'It will get him off your hands, and get him out of danger at the same time,' Jim explained. 'You'll be able to get a good night's sleep again.'

Towards evening Jim took Sharon a creel of turf and a jug of the morning's milk. He found her in the kitchen, cleaning her brushes while studying the oil painting on her easel.

'Can I have a peek?' he asked.

'Peek away.' She turned the easel and the painting towards the window.

He studied the two crude-looking figures on the canvas, not quite knowing what to make of them. The figure on the left had a simian head and a burly, almost shapeless body. The figure next to it was tall and thin with a hard, rocklike face suggesting human features that had been eroded by millennia of rain and rough weather.

'What do you think?' she smiled.

He had to think swiftly because he had no idea what to say. He looked at the roughly made painting again and thought of the Cloigeann, a standing stone on the hill with a bull's head.

'One of the figures reminds me of the Cloigeann but it isn't the Cloigeann. I don't think I ever saw an ape standing next to it.'

'It isn't the Cloigeann, I agree, but the Cloigeann was at the back of my mind. I'm going to call it "The Stone Men".'

'And what is the ape doing next to the rock?'

'Ah, you've got it all wrong. I'll let you in on a secret. I started off painting Red Miller standing next to Muiris and then, as I painted, the whole thing took off in a contrary direction. Now it's no longer Red Miller and Muiris, but I think it says something about a certain type of civilisation that hasn't been said before.'

'You fooled me. But then I'm no connoisseur.'

'Neither am I. I've never met a connoisseur. Have you?'

'I've met one or two but they didn't impress me.'

'You must introduce me some time. Now, since we've got milk, I'll make you a cup of tea.'

He talked to Emily about the picture she was colouring while Sharon went about the kitchen, making slithering noises in her worn-out slippers.

'What are you doing tomorrow?' she asked as she poured the tea.

'If the day is good, I'll spend it on the bog cutting turf.'

'You must sit for me some time if you can find the time. Already I can see the portrait in my mind's eye.'

'It wouldn't work. I'm not Muiris, not the archetypal Man of Leaca.'

'Let me see now?' She came across and cupped his chin in her hand. Then she turned his head so that the dying sunlight fell on his left cheek and temple.

'Yes, that would do. You're younger than Muiris and like him you're tall, and you have the same strong features. When you're his age, I'll paint another portrait of you and then you'll see what I mean.'

'Muiris is a peacock who has no need of peahens. He's self-sufficient, self-righteous and self-opinionated.'

'He's my favourite neighbour. He's the only man in Leaca with my sense of humour. He's got his own way of talking. Everything he says can be taken in ten different ways.'

'You may change your mind if you ever feel the sharp edge of his tongue.' He got up and thanked her for the tea.

'When are you going back to Dublin?' she asked.

'At the weekend. We'll have finished the turf-cutting by then. While I'm here, I'll bring you a creel of turf every day to keep you warm.'

'Do you think Nick will ever come back?' she asked as he went to the door.

'If he has any sense, he will.'

'I can't stay here much longer on my own, I'm afraid.'

'What will you do? Sell the place?'

'Who would buy it? The foxes?'

'Keep it, then. A bolthole in the country is a lovely thing to have.'

He went off down the road with the empty creel on his back, aware that she was watching him from the door. Talking to her had an unsettling effect on him. She was quite unlike any of the girls he'd met in Dublin.

20

*M*uiris took an empty ten-glass whiskey bottle from the dresser and filled it with poteen from an earthenware jar. The poteen was for Jim Barron, whose brand of humour he appreciated. Jim knew how to tell a story, and, what is more, he enjoyed a drop of the real McCoy. Not that he needed the real McCoy to tell a real story for he had a gift not given to everyone. Tom, Jim's father, didn't have it, and neither did his mother. Jim must have got it from listening to Paddy Canty as a boy. Muiris fancied himself as a storyteller. Now that Paddy had gone, he saw himself as the only true shanachie left in Leaca.

It was almost nine o'clock as he pulled on his donkey jacket and headed for Tom Barron's, holding the bottle of poteen by the neck. He hadn't seen much of Tom since they'd disagreed over Ambrose. Now, thankfully, all that was water under the bridge. Tom was a good neighbour, and for that reason he liked to be on good terms with him. He was a proud man was Tom, and like all proud men he couldn't stand pride in anyone else. It was a question of the mountain and Mohammed, and Muiris was a big enough mountain to let bygones be bygones and make his way, however proudly, to Mohammed.

As he turned into Barron's lane, he thought he spied a light where no light should be. At the bend he lost sight of it and thought no more about it. The night was moonless, but the sky was a colander of stars, which was as good as any half-moon, though not as good as a moon at the full. It was what his father used to call a 'sky-moon night'. The stars were blinking though there was no hint of frost. It was a sign of dry weather to come, just what was needed for the turf-cutting. When Jim and Tom had finished their own turf-cutting, they might give a good neighbour a start, but he wouldn't ask them, he'd allow them to do the decent thing of their own accord. That way they'd feel they'd done him a good turn out of the goodness of their hearts. Now that Ambrose had gone, help was not easy to come by. If Tom and Jim didn't give him a hand, he'd have to pay a youth from the lower glen.

As he rounded the crook of the lane, he saw light in the old house, and between him and the clear night sky a thread of smoke rising from the chimney. It was all very strange. Was Tom making a run of poteen on the sly? Highly unlikely. He was a cautious man, not a man to risk being caught on the wrong side of the law. Keeping to the grass verge, he approached the window of the old house but a heavy curtain blocked his view. He went round the side and looked in through the back window at the two men who were seated on either side of the fireplace. He stayed looking for several minutes because he could not believe his eyes. Then he turned on his heel and went back down the lane still clutching his bottle of poteen.

'It's hard to believe,' Cormac said.

'You may well believe it,' Muiris snorted. 'I saw him sitting by the fire in the old house with my own two eyes. At first I didn't recognise him for the beard.'

He reached into a niche in the fireplace wall and pulled out a fistful of dried dillisk, a purple seaweed, which he distributed among the four neighbours whom he'd invited at short notice. They all began chewing the dillisk as if it were betel or the choicest Virginia tobacco leaf. They were well used to chewing dillisk or dulse, which had a slightly salty flavour and provoked the desire for another glass of Muiris's excellent poteen. Pouring generously, Muiris handed a brimming glass to each of them. To fulfil the requirements of long-established custom, he made a hot toddy for himself before returning to his armchair in the chimney corner.

'He was sitting by the fire talking to Jim,' he said. 'There was a *sráideog* on the floor by the fire for Ambrose to sleep on. He had his back to me but still I recognised him. It was the slope of the shoulders and the small hands that gave him away.'

'Could he be a friend of Jim's down from Dublin for a day or two?' Red Miller wondered.

'Why should a friend of Jim's be wearing Ambrose's green jacket?' Muiris demanded.

They all looked at one another as the true import of Muiris's question sank in.

'It doesn't make sense,' Marcus said. 'Why should Tom give him quarters with the police looking for him in every port?'

'Tom goes his own way, he was always deep,' Muiris emphasised. 'He knew about the Triangle. Maybe he's trying to save him from his rightful fate.'

'It's a curious thing for a good neighbour to do,' Neil Durkin pronounced.

'It's hard to credit,' Red Miller said. 'Tom going about his business as usual, while harbouring a wanted man. I was talking to him only this morning on the hill.'

'We've been bamboozled once,' Muiris said. 'We can't allow ourselves to be bamboozled again.'

'What can we do?' Neil Durkin wondered.

'Last time we drew lots, and one of us got the Triangle. None of us knows who got it except the man who drew it. It's up to him to carry out the sentence before anything else can go wrong. Now we all know the score and what is more we know where to find Ambrose. We'll say no more about it tonight. The next time we meet we'll be talking history.'

'You mean we'll be talking about Agent Cox?' Cormac said.

'Agent Cox is history, I agree. Ambrose must join him for the sake of history, too.'

'How will we know the sentence has been carried out?' Neil Durkin asked.

'I'll know,' Muiris said. 'I was fooled once. I'll never be fooled again.'

Red Miller drained his glass and put it down. He was looking into the fire, as if trying to discern the outline of a face in the coals. Muiris reached into the niche in the chimney corner and produced more dillisk. He poured another drink, and they talked about turf-cutting for a while.

'We'll call it a night, men,' Muiris said finally. 'I won't pour another because one of us must stay sober as any judge. There's serious business to be done and tonight is the best time to do it.'

★ ★ ★

Jim felt pleased with himself. He had found a way of getting his father out of a hole and doing himself a favour at the same time. Ambrose had an interesting story to tell, and he had enough savvy to realise that he didn't have the skill to find the right words for readers of a popular newspaper. His story would create a storm. The police would find themselves in the shit, and deservedly so. He would have to be patient, however. First of all Ambrose would have to clear his name and the real culprit must be found. For a moment he wondered if Ambrose was leading him up the garden path but he immediately put the disturbing thought from his mind. He would have to help the poor devil in every way he could. If necessary, he would arrange for him to have the use of a safe house in Dublin where he could live until the hue and cry died down.

He crossed the yard to the barn, where Ambrose was lying on the bed reading a book he'd lent him: Robin

Flower's translation of Tomás Ó Criomhthain's autobiography describing life on the Great Blasket in the second half of the nineteenth century.

'I'm enjoying *The Islandman*,' Ambrose said. 'It's a book that everyone in Leaca should read. The life it describes isn't very far removed from the life we know here.'

'But we have no Tomás Ó Criomhthain now that Paddy Canty has gone.'

Ambrose closed the book. Awkwardly, he got up from the bed and sat on a chair by the fire.

'Have you spoken to Sharon?'

'Yes, I brought her a creel of turf and a jug of milk just now.'

'What did she say?'

'Like everyone else, she thinks you did a bunk to evade the law.'

'I suppose she thinks I'm guilty.'

'I suppose she does.'

'Is she worried about me?'

'Well, naturally.'

'Is she very distressed?'

'I think she's got over the initial shock. She's bearing up.'

'What did she say?' he asked again.

'She said she couldn't stay here on her own much longer. She's thinking of moving to Dublin.'

'And how is Emily?'

'Playing with her doll. She's a lovely little girl.'

'Sharon must think I've deserted them. The sooner I can talk to her the better.'

'You'll have to be patient. You can't talk to her here without giving the game away. You'll have to wait till I manage to get all three of you to Dublin. I've already got a place for you in mind.'

'The move can't come too soon for me.'

'Have you given any thought to our article? It must be hard-hitting. It must show up the police for the bumbling idiots they are.'

'Article? I was thinking of writing a book.'

'But a book will take ages to write! We must publish while the iron is hot, while your name is still hot news. The reading public has a very short memory.'

'I don't see it like that. I've suffered for this. I don't intend frittering away the experience on one or two ephemeral articles.'

'It's a question of money,' Jim reminded him. 'You need to find a way of supporting yourself and your family. You can boil down your experience into two or three articles, and when they've been published and you've pocketed the money, you can turn to your book. That way you'll get a breather to write literary prose. You'll kill two birds with one stone.'

'You could be talking sense there.'

'We mustn't pull our punches. Remember that a good article is an article that someone in authority would rather not see published. We must lay the blame squarely at the door of the police.'

'That isn't how I see it. I was planning to turn it into an analysis of the mores of an isolated rural community.'

'Oh, that would never do.'

'It would really set the cat among the pigeons, though.'

'Wrong cat, wrong pigeons. It would be attacking the soul and culture of the Gaeltacht. You must remember that the Gaeltacht is seen by many as an ideal of Irish life. Any criticism of it wouldn't look good, especially coming from an outsider.'

'I can only write the truth as I see it,' Ambrose said, rather pompously, he thought.

'It's horses for courses. You write it as you see it, then, and I'll rewrite it for popular consumption. After that you'll be free to rejig it as you like for your book. My editor always says that if you find the right angle, you've found your story. I think he's right. The angle makes both the story and the moral of the story.'

'And isn't that why all journalism is shit! I think I'd better sleep on this,' Ambrose said.

Jim got up to go. Ambrose was being awkward and he knew it. Jim couldn't help wondering if his plan to get some good copy out of him would ever work. He didn't have a choice, though. The first requirement was to find a way out of the cul-de-sac his father had woven for himself. The business of money was secondary. Still, he would jot down a structure for Ambrose's articles in order to keep him on the straight and narrow.

'I hope you don't mind if I lock the door.'

'I do mind. If you lock it, I'll feel imprisoned. Surely, you can trust me. With the police on my tail, I have nothing to gain by running away.'

'As you wish,' Jim said, without adding a 'good night.'

Ambrose felt tired and out of sorts. He had been wondering if Jim would ever leave. Jim was a typical journalist with an eye to nothing except the main chance. Still, he couldn't afford to turn up his nose at his offer. He would write his story, giving just the bare bones. Then Jim could edit and publish it under his own byline. He would save the best things for his book, however. That way the essence of his experience would not be vulgarised by a man bent on titillating sensationalism for the masses.

He lay down on the bed and picked up the book again. After a few minutes he closed his eyes. Sharon was on his mind, and Jim had been less than frank. He knew more than he was letting on. There was only one thing for it. He would have to pay her a visit. Even if he told her the ghastly truth, she wouldn't think any the less of him. Nothing could be worse than not knowing and wondering why and where he'd gone. Sharon was not a placid person. She craved movement and excitement. Already she'd be making plans for a life without him. That was why he must see her straightaway. It was almost eleven. He would wait until the neighbours were asleep, and make sure to be back in his bed before first light.

Again he went over his conversation with Jim, an intelligent man who lacked the instinct for objective analysis. This wasn't a story about the incompetence of the police. It was a story that had its roots in a colonial past and the prejudices of an inbred community against an innocent stranger cast in the role of the ancient enemy. He had been misled by his neighbours' fondness for company and conversation. And he'd had no idea of the malign influence that one man can have on a whole townland. He had seen Muiris as a consummate actor who would make a run of poteen in the deep mountains today and go out with a shepherd's crook tomorrow, dressed up as Shackleton on his way to the Antarctic. His most arresting memory of him was the day he emerged from the still-house shrouded in smoke and clutching a bottle of the still-warm poteen. Then it had occurred to him that there was something about him that did not belong to the ordinary, everyday world his neighbours knew. Yet he was a man who had earned the respect and concurrence of those around him. For a moment he tried to imagine the kind of man he would be if he had been born in London of good parents who could afford to give him an education to match his keenly critical intelligence.

His neighbours saw him as a kind of seer. Some said that he had *fios,* or prophetic knowledge, and Muiris was not reluctant to play the part. Cormac said that he'd once seen him chew his thumb like the great Fionn Mac Cumhaill to discover the result of a match between Cavan and Mayo a week in advance of the game. Muiris himself claimed to have what he called 'the cure'. Whenever an animal fell sick, people did not send for the vet. Instead, they went to Muiris as a first port of call for advice. In his second week in Leaca he had seen him perform a charm called *snaidhm na péiste* on Paddy Canty's sick cow. Muiris got a piece of string and, holding it over the cow, tied the ends loosely into a series of intricate knots. Then he pulled on both ends of the string and the knots undid themselves with magical ease.

'It came out. She'll get better,' he said to Paddy.

'You never failed me yet,' Paddy replied. 'You're as good as any priest and better than the most expensive vet in the county.'

When he first arrived in Leaca, he had found Muiris and his ancient lore amusing. Now he had come to realise the alarming truth about the man. It wouldn't surprise him if he had murdered Paddy Canty. He remembered Paddy's swollen face, the incredulous look in his eyes, and the wide-open mouth as if he were screaming in silence. If only he could describe that horrifying scene to Sharon and the effect it had on him, she would make a painting to out-Munch Edvard Munch.

Though he had lived in Leaca for over two years, he had to admit that he still knew nothing about his neighbours. Sharon, for all her blind spots, had taken their measure. She had a mind of almost mathematical precision, which meant that she was never in any doubt. When she made a painting, her effects were carefully calculated, whereas he himself lived and wrote in mysteries and uncertainties. Now as he looked back, his whole life seemed shrouded in November fog. There were no clear skies, no distinct outlines. Even his childhood was a haze on a misty autumn morning. Sometimes he attributed this vagueness to the death of his parents when he was just a child. His grandmother did her best for him but nothing would ever be the same again. Soon he became accustomed to living with the makeshift and the imperfect.

On discovering that his first girlfriend was being unfaithful to him with his best friend, he did not fall out with her. Already he knew that betrayal was to be a fact of his life, and when she became ill with cancer, it was he, not his friend, who went to comfort her in the evenings. Looking down at her blank, unseeing face in the open coffin, he realised why she had undervalued him. At that moment he knew he could no longer continue to invent advertising slogans for products he'd never think of buying, but he could not begin to imagine what else he might do instead. Everything changed overnight when he met Sharon. It was she who pointed out the way, who made him see clearly who and what he was. From talking to her he knew within minutes that he was an artist. She fired him with impossible yearnings. No wonder the early years of their relationship were idyllic, at least from his point of view.

He must have slept. He woke in darkness. The fire had died down and the oil lamp had gone out. It was already after one; the neighbours would now be in their beds. He dressed without relighting the lamp in case it might attract attention. It was a night of low cloud with a chilly breeze from the east. Unsteadily, he made his way down the lane. He felt weak at the knees and his head swam dangerously. Sharon would be delighted to see him, but what would she think of him in his present condition? He could not tell her the whole humiliating story. He would have to explain that Jim Barron had promised to be their saviour, and that he had offered to find a safe house for them in Dublin. He would rouse her by scratching at the bedroom window and give her the surprise of her life. Her bed would be warm and he would hold her lovingly in his arms for an hour. He hoped that the ordeal he'd been through would not affect his performance because she was not the kind of girl who would be happy with an apology or excuse. One of her jokes was that the only excuse she accepted was death. As he turned the corner below the cottage, he thought he saw a light in the bedroom. When he drew closer, he realised that the light was in the kitchen, which was strange, given the lateness of the hour.

He went to the window but he could not see through the curtain. He could hear voices inside and he did not know what to make of them. He thought it best not to open the door in case he might give too much away. He found himself shivering uncontrollably from the cold. He opened the barn door and stood inside in the darkness, wondering what he should do. Then the door of the cottage opened and Jim Barron stood for a moment in the lamplight. Sharon took his hand and held it.

'See you tomorrow evening,' he said lightly. She closed the door against the night, as his retreating footsteps echoed on the stony road.

Nick remained in the barn for several minutes, so wounded in spirit that he could hardly breathe. He stood there helplessly, rooted to the earthen floor, as a wave of nausea swept over him, causing him to bend down and grasp his knees. The light in the kitchen went out and the whole house was in darkness like all the other houses around. He could not say how long he'd stood there. Finally roused by the squeak of a rat scrabbling over the potato heap behind him, he emerged without a sound and made his way back to Tom Barron's barn.

Feeling as if he had been beaten on the legs with a stick, he took off his jacket and trousers and pulled the bedclothes up under his chin. He had left on his woollen pullover because of the deeply probing cold. He had always known that Sharon was a woman of strong, even gross, appetites. She could not go without a man for more than a day or two at any one time. At a pinch Paul Flynn, Jim Barron, or indeed any one in trousers would do. It was how she was made, but knowing that was no comfort in his hour of need.

He was looking up at the dark rafters when he realised that he was not alone in the room.

'Who's there?' he called.

A torch shone straight into his eyes but he could not see who was holding it. The torchlight began moving towards him from the far end of the room.

'Is that you, Jim?' he said, sitting up. 'Answer me. What do you want?'

There was no answer and no sound. The light kept moving slowly. Suddenly, he knew the end had come. He got out of bed and made a grab for the torch. Two powerful arms surrounded him. Within seconds his assailant was behind him, one arm pinning both his, and the other pressing against his throat. The man was wearing oilskins, and he reeked of dried sweat. It was a smell he recognised from having worked alongside him many times.

'Red Miller,' he croaked. 'Let me go.'

A big hand tightened on his windpipe. His mouth opened and his tongue shot forward. He tried to scream and couldn't. As he struggled unavailingly to break free, he cursed the weakness in his trunk and limbs. Out of the darkness came a vision of Paddy Canty's last face, a picture of inexpressible panic and horror.

21

*W*hen Jim went out to the barn the following morning, he found the bed empty and the bedclothes strewn all over the floor. A torch lay beside an overturned chair, and next to it, Ambrose's trousers and green jacket. He alerted his father and mother, who said she'd always known that nothing good would come of it all. The two of them stood aghast by the barn door, taking in the scene of chaos and confusion.

'It looks as if there's been a violent struggle,' Jim observed.

'Ambrose was strong. It must have taken an even stronger man to get the better of him, but the fasting would have weakened him, of course,' Tom said.

'You're all very knowledgeable now it's too late,' Nancy said. 'It's high time you told the guards.'

Tom stooped to pick up the torch.

'No, don't! It may have the culprit's fingerprints on it.' Jim pulled a handkerchief from his pocket and wrapped the torch in it.'

'What do you intend doing with it?' his father asked.

'Nothing at present. I'm just concerned to do the sensible thing.'

'You'll have to take it to the barracks,' his mother said. 'Who knows, it may be the very thing the guards are looking for.'

'Could he have met the fate we were trying to save him from?' Jim wondered.

We don't really know,' Tom said. 'He's a clever bucko. He could be trying to put us off the scent.'

'You mean he's gone out over the hill?'

'It isn't impossible.'

'He wouldn't have gone without his jacket and trousers. And what about the torch? I don't think it belonged to him.'

'You'd better take it to the barracks right away, Jim,' his mother said, appealingly.

'It would only get us into trouble. We'd have to admit to holding Ambrose while the police were searching for him. We ourselves would be arrested and charged.'

'We'd better put the place in order,' Tom said. 'If anyone sees it as it is, we'll have a lot of explaining to do.'

They spent an hour or more getting the old kitchen to look like a barn in use. They removed the shakedown and the bedclothes, and cleared the fireplace of embers and ashes. They removed the chairs and also the curtain from the front window.

'We've done all we can, and it's too fine a day to waste,' Jim said when they'd finished. 'We'd better make a start on the turf-cutting.'

Throughout the afternoon, they worked in silence, each absorbed in cheerless thought. They paused around three and sat in the lea of a turf stack to eat a meal of buttered soda bread, hardboiled eggs and sweetened tea.

'What do you think happened? Jim asked.

'I'm sure he's gone the way of Agent Cox,' Tom said. 'I thought we'd outwitted them but Muiris must have tumbled to what was going on.'

'It's hard to believe that something so terrible occurred here in Leaca in this day and age.'

'You don't know Muiris. His word is law this side of Loch an Aifrinn.'

'Someone murdered Paddy Canty. Maybe it was Ambrose after all.'

'If it was, it might give us some peace of mind, but somehow I doubt it.'

Neither of them spoke for a while. Tom got his pipe going and Jim lit a cigarette.

'If you're lucky, you can go through life without ever being really tested,' Tom said. 'I was tested at the eleventh hour when I least expected it. As it happened, it was the wrong test for me. I always saw myself as someone who dealt fairly and squarely with every other man. I'll no longer be able to shave on Sunday morning without thinking that the man in the mirror is not the real man at all.'

'You mustn't blame yourself. We all failed Ambrose in our own separate ways.'

The following day Jim ran into Cormac returning from the hill with a motherless lamb in a back-creel. 'Any news of Ambrose?' he asked with a superior smile.

'As far as I know, the police are still looking for him.'

'They won't find him where he's gone.' Cormac spoke with a knowing tilt of the head.

'You mean he's in another country?' Jim probed.

'I suppose you could call it that.'

'He was a hard man to fathom,' Jim said to prolong the conversation.

'No one is transparent. People do the strangest things, people you'd think would know better.'

'We live in an upside-down world.'

'That's what Paddy Canty used to say, poor man. I hope he's at peace now. Isn't that what we all hope and pray for?'

He left Cormac to his pious thoughts. He was one of those men who liked to be seen to be in the know. Over dinner he told his father what Cormac had been hinting at.

'Not one of the Gildeas could keep a secret,' his father said. 'I was talking to Daniel earlier. Cormac was even more explicit with him. There's no doubt about it. Ambrose is dead and buried on the mountain with Agent Cox. Daniel said Cormac couldn't contain his glee. "He won't be lonely.

He'll have someone to talk to. They both spoke the same language, don't you know." Believe it or not, that was what he said.'

Standing by the corner of the window, Sharon watched Jim coming up the road, shoulders straining under the weight of the heavy creel. He was a good neighbour. He had brought her a creel of black turf and a jug of milk every evening since he came home. One evening just before bedtime he came armed with half a bottle of Jameson, which had led her to believe that he had great things in mind. He was an amusing conversationalist and something of a storyteller, while managing to give the impression that making an impression was the last thing on his mind.

They talked for a while about their favourite Jack Yeats paintings, and how impossible it was to see everything you'd like to see. He told her about one or two Dublin critics who wrote about contemporary art, which gave her the idea that he was a man with influential friends. Unlike Nick, she was hard headed. She knew that talent wasn't everything. You needed luck and charm, and the knack to make the best of any opportunity that came your way. Jim was the kind of man who could point her in the right direction.

When they'd done for the whiskey, she sat on his knee, thinking that she might tease him, just a little. She had expected him to try to kiss her but he kept talking as if she were still sitting on the other side of the fire. They must have talked for two hours. It was after one when he left. She'd told herself at the time that he was shy, but perhaps he was playing a waiting game. Some men were as devious as any woman. She couldn't help feeling that he was the kind of man it would take a long time to get to know.

He left the creel sitting on the wall of the yard and came in with the jug of milk. He was the only one of her neighbours who knocked before entering, and that was something she appreciated. She could tell from the heat of the jug that the milk had come straight from the cow.

'It's this evening's milk,' he said. 'It's been strained but it hasn't had time to cool.'

She put a saucer over the jug before placing it on the window-sill.

'I'm busy packing,' she said. 'I had a letter from a friend in Dublin. He's found us a place to stay, at least for the time being.'

'When are you leaving?'

'Tomorrow, if I can. There's nothing to keep me here any longer.'

He said that he would be going back on Saturday and that he'd give her a lift, provided she was willing to travel light. 'It's my Anglia,' he explained. 'A bit cramped, I'm afraid.'

She gave him tea and a biscuit. He seemed somewhat crestfallen. He wasn't his usual talkative self.

'I've given up on Nick,' she said. 'You'd think he'd have written by now.'

'Writing isn't easy if you're on the run, I suppose.'

'I'm sure he could have sent a message via one of our Dublin friends.'

'Maybe he doesn't trust them. Have you thought of that?'

'I've thought and thought. I've done little else but think since he left. He wasn't an easy man to know, but I refuse to believe he was a murderer. I suppose I shouldn't talk about him in the past tense, but that's how I see him. Somehow I don't think he'll ever come back.'

'Why do you say that?' he asked seriously.

'We never really got to know each other. He didn't know what to make of me and I didn't know what to make of him.'

'But you were happy together?'

'Well, yes, I suppose we were. He was absorbed in his writing and I was absorbed in my painting. We kept each other company, and most of the time that was all either of us needed. Now I know precisely how much Emily and I meant to him. Imagine walking out like that without a word. I'm sorry, I just don't understand it.'

He sat looking into the fire as if he had not heard. Perhaps he did not want her to talk about Nick, though she'd always felt that he and Nick got on well together. On his visits home he used to lend Nick the odd book. It was he who introduced them to the short stories of Liam O'Flaherty, which they both enjoyed.

'Do you live on your own in Dublin?' She thought she'd try a change of subject.

'Yes, I have a flat in Sandymount.'

'I'll be staying in Donnybrook, just down the road. It would be nice to keep in touch.'

'Yes, it would. As ex-residents of Leaca, we'd have something in common, I suppose.' For a moment he looked as if he was about to make a witty comment, but he gazed into the fire again as if he'd forgotten what he was about to say.

'Have you finished the turf-cutting?' She tried a different tack.

'Just about. Another hour or two will chase the hare.'

'Chase the hare?'

'It's our way of saying that we'll get shut of it.'

'You must be pleased.'

'I'm tired.' He smiled wearily.

'Does Leaca always have this effect on you?'

'I come back to regain perspective. Things that loom large in Dublin have no meaning here.'

'Is the reverse also true?'

'Not for me. The things that matter to me here matter even more in Dublin. Leaca follows me around but Dublin doesn't.'

'I knew you were a true Leaca man. That's why I wanted to do a portrait of you.'

'You can do it in Dublin but not here.'

'I'd like to paint you with your turf-spade on your shoulder, wearing knee-straps just like Muiris.'

'You wouldn't want to paint a lie. It would show only one face of the cube.'

He smiled at her as he got up to go.

'What time will you be leaving on Saturday?' she asked as he reached the door.

'I'll call down after breakfast. We'll leave around ten.'

He had felt awkward talking to her. Escaping was a blessing and sheer relief. Wherever he turned he was reminded of Ambrose. That morning he had run into Muiris on the way to the bog. Muiris was wearing his green donkey jacket, and leather knee-straps to keep the cuffs of his trousers from getting dirty. No matter where he was or what he was doing, he contrived to look different from anyone else around. Unlike the other locals, he enjoyed dressing up. He shaved every day and kept his white moustache neatly trimmed.

'I thought you said you'd be coming down to see me. I've saved a very special bottle for you.'

'I'll come down this evening, if that's all right.'

'Why wouldn't it? I have a story to tell you.'

'How do you know I haven't heard it already?' He thought he'd try a little dart of ambiguity.

'Because I made it up myself. It's as fresh as an egg straight from a hen's behind, and as perfect. Nothing beats a story that's never been told before.'

'I prefer old stories, ones that are well polished from retelling.'

Muiris drew himself up to his full height and held out his crook to the full length of his arm. He looked every inch a man of acknowledged authority and, furthermore, a man who knew the value of the symbols of high office.

'I'll tell you two stories, then, a new story and an old story. *Scéal úr agus sean scéal.* And while we're at it, we'll drink a toast to absent friends.' His lower jaw trembled as he bared his teeth in silent laughter. Jim raised his hand in farewell. Was one story about Agent Cox, and the other about Nick Ambrose?'

'How is Her Ladyship?' his mother asked when he returned from seeing Sharon.

'Bearing up, I think. She won't die of grief.'

'You didn't tell her the truth, did you?'

'No, the truth would be too terrible for her to bear.'

'That isn't why you didn't tell her.' His mother looked up sharply from her knitting.

'I met Muiris on the hill this morning. He invited me down this evening.' He thought he might try to wean away her mind from Sharon.

'You're not going to see him after what he did!'

'He said he had something to give me.'

'Poteen, what else? He just wants a hand with the turf. Well, I wouldn't please him.'

'Like everyone else, Muiris has a good side as well as a bad side. He'd have made an excellent journalist, if only he'd had half a chance.'

'He's guilty of murder.'

'If he is, he doesn't show it. Like my editor, he's devoid of all moral scruples.'

'You mean he doesn't know the difference between right and wrong?'

'Something like that.'

'He knows only too well but he doesn't let it trouble him. I wouldn't like to be in his two big boots on Judgment Day.'

One of his mother's strong points was that she always knew what to think. Like Muiris, she did not know the meaning of doubt.

'I'd better not tell him that.' Smiling, he reached for his cap.

Tom Barron was standing on the cliff edge, looking out to sea. The wind from the land was skimming froth off the crests of the waves, which rode in one after the other, rising over rocks and spilling back in white rivulets to be swallowed up again by the waves that followed. He found a kind of comfort in the forever-and-ever motion of restless water, in things happening naturally, seabirds crying below and the clouds above hurrying into the west.

'Expecting cast-in, Tom?' It was Daniel, the schoolmaster, who spoke.

'Just noticing things I've seen a thousand times before.'

'I'm the same. I like looking at things Adam must have noticed long ago in the garden. There's peace of mind in little things, and these days we need all the peace we can get.'

'It's a terrible business, Daniel. It has a lobster's grip on my mind.'

'If only we'd taken the threat more seriously, maybe we could have stopped it happening.'

'I took it seriously enough, God knows. I thought about it night and day. I just couldn't see my way out of the fog.'

'Thinking isn't enough,' Daniel said. 'We both knew what we should do, but we weren't strong enough to do it. It's a shocking comment on the limitations of two serious men.'

'It was like sailing through a narrow channel between two big rocks. If you veer too much to one side or the other you make matchwood of your boat.'

'With hindsight, we should have told the police,' Daniel said. 'If we had, it would not be on our conscience today.'

'What must we do now?' Tom wondered.

'I think we should both tell McNally what happened. Then it will be up to him to bring the culprits to justice.'

'It wouldn't help poor Ambrose, and it would only cause ill feeling. We'd be the talk of the three parishes. We wouldn't be able to hold up our heads in the chapel or on a fair day ever again.'

'The alternative is to live with it, and that isn't easy either.'

'Give me a bit of time, and I'll think about it,' Tom said. 'I'll talk to Nancy when the time is ripe for talk.'

Daniel headed south along the cliffs, hoping to enjoy one of his favourite views, standing with his back to the perfect stonework of the Tower looking out towards the island and the white lighthouse on the far side of the bay. Today he walked briskly with the breeze on his left cheek, but still he could not put behind him the terrible events that soured the very earth underfoot. How could they have happened in the community he knew and loved? Or thought he knew. Ambrose may have been a nuisance but he was an innocent, a lamb in the middle of a wolf pack. Having come to Leaca to seek peace and renewal, poor man, he saw nothing but good in men who'd led him to believe that he was being received with open arms. Was the fault in the inbred culture from which the little mountain community drew its strength, or was there a pervasive poison in the mountain air? Taken individually, his neighbours were honest, upright men whose only thought was wresting a living from soil and sea; but in what you might call 'conference', their darker nature surfaced. It was as if each had activated a splinter of wickedness in the heart of the others until it burgeoned and tainted every thought and action.

No one could escape blame. He himself could not. Neither could Tom Barron, a man who seemed at pains to do only what was right. Even Tom did not seem to grasp the extent of their culpability or the enormity of what had taken place. Taken place? The phrase was inadequate to describe a crime in which every man in Leaca had played a part. It was as if the collective demands of the tribe had obliterated all individual feelings of humanity, morality, decency and responsibility. He felt deeply ashamed of himself, so ashamed that he dared not tell Sheila everything he knew. Waking from his reverie, he found himself looking down at a white wave swirling round the base of Tor a' Chreasaigh, a noble sea stack cleansed daily by salty wind and water, but not even a tidal wave would now cleanse the acid soil of Leaca.

Heading back the way he had come, he stood on the stony beach where generations of fishermen had hauled their boats and counted and shared their catch. To him it had been a place made sacred by honest toil. He stooped to pick up a white stone the size of a goose egg from among the stones at his feet. Weighing it in his right hand, he caressed its surface with his thumb as if to seek tactile comfort from an object indifferent to either good or evil. The surface of the stone was worn smooth but its curve was still not perfect. On one side was just a hint of a swelling, which was not quite visible to the eye. He flung the gibbous missile into the water with such force that he almost lost his balance.

'What were you aiming at?' Neil Durkin came up behind him.

'The sea, of course.'

'Well, at least you didn't miss,' he smiled

'I wasn't trying to.'

'They say Cuchulainn fought the waves. He must have been mad to take on the sea.'

'Maybe he had reason to be mad.'

'People do strange things at times. I once saw Ambrose standing on the spot you're on now, throwing one stone after another into the sea. "What are you doing?" says I. "Trying to find out how long it will take the sea to cast them up again," says he. Sure, that man had a screw loose. He used to do the oddest things.'

'There's room for all sorts in God's plentiful world,' Daniel said.

'Is there room for murderers, I wonder?'

'We'll all be judged one day, guilty and innocent, murderer and victim, alike.'

'Muiris says that too much reading will soften a man's brain.'

'Well, Muiris need have no fear of that. He's always boasting that *Old Moore's Almanac* is the only book in his house.'

'I'm going to try a few shots of the hand-line from the Leic Chrochta,' Neil Durkin said. 'There's nothing like fishing to put a man's thoughts in their proper order and place.'

Daniel raised his hand and turned on his heel. All his life he had lived contentedly in Leaca, drawing strength from the living culture of its little community. He had seen it as an open community, generous and warm-hearted to a fault. It was a community in which both stranger and beggar were always made welcome. Now one determined man had changed all that. Or had a deformed history of injustice and misery also taken a hand? If Agent Cox had not been murdered, Ambrose would be alive today. It was a case of false parallels born out of ignorance and superstition. So what must he do? Go to the police and spill beans that were not his to spill? The police were bound to meet with a wall of silence. There was no proof, only nods, winks, hearsay and supposition. Instead he would talk to Sheila about moving. Leaca was a void, an empty bottle that had once contained an animating liquor. He couldn't live out the rest of his days in a place of moral nullity.

★ ★ ★

Standing in the centre of the Leic Chrochta, Neil Durkin unwound his hand-line, making sure it fell cleanly at his feet. He had been busy all week on a web for the factory in Kilcar. This was his first attempt at fishing since Sunday. He had come because he needed to be alone with the sea for an hour, to allow the sediment in his thoughts to settle, and to think without having to try to think. He could tell what Daniel was up to: talking about Judgment Day to make him feel guilty. Muiris was right. Too much reading makes shit of the brain. Daniel probably felt guilty himself and wanted to steep everyone else in the same pickle. He'd got too close to Ambrose, lending him books and reading his poems. That would explain his difficulty. And being the type of man he was, he'd like everyone else to feel the same. It was like that fake story of the fox that lost his tail. He himself didn't feel any guilt. Why should he? He didn't murder Paddy Canty and he didn't murder Ambrose. He minded his own business, which was warping, filling bobbins and weaving. He was a good weaver. Given the right thread, he could turn out a web with any man in the parish. The last batch of thread wasn't as good as it should have been. The weft kept breaking and holding him up. Unlike some weavers he could name, he didn't lose his temper and curse the factory manager. He took his time because what mattered was a job well done. A man was no more and no less than his work when every copper was counted. That's where Ambrose had gone wrong. He had no real work he could call his own. Writing isn't work, and neither is stealing eggs and turf. Not real work. Not work you could feel proud of. You couldn't say at the end of the day, 'That's a job well done.'

He shot the line and waited a few seconds for the lead to sink. He hauled slowly and carefully, giving the line an occasional jerk while making sure it didn't wet his only pair of trousers. Daniel needed watching. No one knew his mind or even what he'd do next. He probably thought everyone felt guilty like himself. In a situation like this, a man had to be careful. He had to keep his thoughts in order, and not allow them to run away with him. An orderly mind meant content-ment and peace; it was a blessing from heaven. And what more could any man ask for? Of course, he needed the company of other people from time to time. He couldn't live entirely on his own. Tom Barron had Nancy and Daniel had Sheila, but he himself had no one to talk to in bed at night. That's why he would have to be careful and not let his thoughts run riot. The sound of the sea was as good a cure as any. Whenever he felt the pressure building up inside his head after a long day at the loom, he would take his fishing-rod from under the eaves, and after ten minutes on the Leic Chrochta he'd feel as right as rain again. The sight and sound of moving water was better than a visit to the doctor—the noise of waves breaking and lapping and licking, and spilling over the rocks and then running off the rocks back into the sea. You could predict a good tune on the fiddle or the melodeon if you knew a right note from a wrong one, but no one could predict the music of the sea because no two waves ever broke with the same force and sound, and all the waves taken together never made the same sound from one minute to the next.

If only Ambrose had realised that, he'd have been a happier man. In many ways he was better off dead. Leaca was certainly a better place without him. Now everyone could sleep sound of a night. Sadly, there would be less need for meetings with Muiris, and less opportunity to sample the best poteen on the west coast of Ireland. Muiris was as solid as the Rock of Gibraltar or even the Tor Mór itself. A little charge of excitement ran up his arm and down his spine. He began hauling in the line with both hands, seeking to gauge the size of the fish by its resistance. It was a fine wee pollock with a rounded belly. Its slithery, greenish-brown sides reminded him of the colour of wrack. He felt happy and at peace with the world. Fishing had the same effect on the mind that a plane has on rough-sawn timber. It could make smooth the knottiest of thoughts.

Red Miller's arrest a month later created anger and confusion among the men of Leaca. At first everyone thought he had been arrested for the murder of Nick Ambrose, but gradually it emerged that he had been charged with the murder of Paddy Canty. The subsequent trial was reported by Jim Barron in the newspaper and in greater detail in the local paper, all of which created a great stir in Leaca. For several weeks it was the only subject of conversation in every chimney corner, and Daniel Burke was in great demand for his skill in translating and interpreting the lawyers' questions and arguments for his eager neighbours. When Red Miller was found guilty and sentenced to nineteen years' imprisonment, there was general incredulity in the townland.

'You'd never think Red Miller was a murderer, now would you?' Cormac said.

'I still don't believe it,' his friend Marcus said in support. 'Red Miller is a rough man but he isn't a bad man.'

'Maybe we all made a terrible mistake.' Neil Durkin pursed his lips and shook his head.

'No one made a mistake,' Muiris declared. 'It was just the contrariness of too many things happening to go wrong at the same time. Who could have foreseen Tom Barron's underhand game? *Uisce faoi thalamh.* There's nothing worse.'

Neil Durkin did not challenge Muiris directly, but over the coming weeks he mentioned his unease again and again to his other neighbours. While no one was willing to question his own role in the tragedy, everyone was prepared to cast about for a plausible excuse, or better still, a scapegoat. Cormac blamed Muiris's poteen, and his friend Marcus Quinn was inclined to agree. He said that it was like no poteen he'd ever tasted. It was smoother than normal poteen, with the result that you did not know how much of it you were drinking. Quite possibly, Muiris had a personal grudge against Ambrose, and the poteen was his way of getting everyone else to agree with him.

Cormac said that he wouldn't be surprised if that were true. There was something dark, even sinister, about Muiris. He was the kind of man you wouldn't like to meet on a lonely road on a moonless night. Sharon, Cormac noted, had spotted the evil in his eye. The paintings she made of him were not like the paintings she made of anyone else in Leaca. Gradually the idea took hold that Muiris had led them all astray. They stopped meeting at his house in the evenings and instead gathered for easeful conversation at Neil Durkin's. Unfortunately, Neil did not have a plentiful supply of poteen on offer. At first they saw it as an inconvenience, but after a while they became accustomed to the new regime.

Muiris was too proud to give anyone cause to think that he had noticed any change in their routines. He kept himself to himself, seeking neither help nor approbation from any other man. He and Tom Barron remained aloof from each other. Whenever they met on the hill they would nod and say good day, but that was as far as their relationship would stretch.

'I suppose a sort of justice has been done,' Tom said to Daniel one day on the hill. 'At least the murderer is now behind bars.'

'No matter how much we try to explain things, we can never make amends. And isn't that the essence of the tragedy?' Daniel replied.

'As you say, the badness is done. We can't unbake the cake.'

'Life will never again be the same in Leaca. I don't think I want to grow old here. The very ground we walk on is poison.'

'You're lucky, you can begin a new life somewhere else. The rest of us must live among these rocks and hills. In every place I ever talked to Ambrose, I'll hear his voice in my ear crying out against the wrong we did him.'

'The more I think about it, the more I blame our misconceived loyalty to the tribe,' Daniel said. 'Our politicians boast about having fought for Irish freedom, but none of us will be free till all tribal loyalties and tribal prejudices go the way of last year's snows.'

Tom didn't quite know what Daniel meant, and he did not pursue the question. All he knew was that Daniel was unhappy. He himself felt uneasy with Nancy. The knowledge that he had failed to live up to her idea of him, and the sense of humiliation he was condemned to endure, pursued him both inside and outside the house. She spent hours on her knees praying for him, and that troubled him as much as the senseless death of Nick Ambrose. He thought of him morning and evening. There was no peace, no ease, no time of self-forgetfulness. All that was left to him was his work, and he wondered what he'd do when he could work no longer. A withering blight had fallen on his life, and every day that passed reminded him of the evil in the heart of man.

Jim Barron did his best not to dwell unduly on his own role in the tragedy. He tried to convince himself that painful stories formed the warp and weft of his working life, many of them at least as distressing as the story of Nick Ambrose. It was his job as a journalist to report them, and to do that effectively he could not allow himself to become emotionally involved in any of them. He had to cultivate objectivity, even if it meant growing a thicker skin than the next man. His editor took the view that a well-written story was one than had the minimum effect on the writer and the maximum effect on the reader. He had done his best to view the story of Ambrose as he would any other story, but somehow he could not uproot it from the fertile loam of his imagination. It still kept burgeoning, pestering him at all hours. He would go to bed thinking about it, and sometimes he would wake up thinking about it. He would hurry to the office, hoping that he would get some all-absorbing story to investigate that would finally displace the story of Ambrose and allow him to get on with his life in peace.

Over the months he discovered that he and Sharon had several friends in common. Socially, she was much in demand. She was good-looking and easy to talk to, and she did not take herself too seriously. He kept running into her at parties. She rarely mentioned Nick, but somehow he could never feel at ease with her. It was as if she and he had known each other in circumstances that neither of them wished to recall.

On his occasional visits home he could not but be aware of the growing infirmity of his parents and their neighbours. Over the years he watched them all grow old. Muiris was the saddest case. He lost his memory and took to wandering the hills alone at all hours. He never seemed to take the direct route anywhere. If he wished to go north, he'd set out in an easterly direction and gradually veer round towards his destination, as if his whole objective was to postpone the moment of arrival. One January morning he was found frozen on the shore of Loch an Aifrinn within sight of his old still-house.

Daniel moved to Donegal Town and never returned. Tom, his father, died from a stroke, and his mother did not live long after him. Red Miller died of heart failure while still in prison. For a few years Neil Durkin was the only resident left in Leaca. Then one day the postman found him dead at his loom.

Gradually, the roads and laneways became overgrown, and tufts of grass and rushes sprang from the once golden thatch of the cottages. In the late 1980s Jim Barron returned out of a desire to see the old place once again. Leaca now had the look of a hamlet that had been deserted a long, long time ago. He parked his car and walked from house to house, pausing outside each to remember its former inhabitants. He entered his parents' house and sat in his father's armchair by the now cold fireplace. Then he sat in his mother's chair, the chair in which she used to knit him socks and cable-stitch pullovers. They were good people, he thought, who lived good lives that had been blighted towards the end, and that, too, was a tragedy.

He heard his father's resonant voice again as he lit his pipe that day on the bog. 'I always saw myself as a good-living man but I'm no longer the man I thought I knew.'

Sadly, he would never finish his book on the old oral culture of Leaca. He had filled four copybooks with his father's stories and sayings, and seven copybooks with those of Muiris and Paddy Canty. It was to be a labour of love, a book to celebrate that part of his experience that was more precious to him than anything else in his life. In all, he had written over half a million words, but he could not find the will to knock them into the shape he envisaged. Whenever he faced the task, the image of Ambrose rose up before him like a boulder in a river that deflects the natural course of the water. Again and again, he had sought a way round the impediment, only to be confronted by a failure of the imagination and a paralysis of the will itself. He could not bring himself to tell the whole truth, and he wouldn't be happy telling only half the truth.

He went for a walk on the cliffs and sat looking down on the Stuaic and Bud a' Diabhail, on cormorants coming and going while seagulls wheeled and glided over his head. He thought of Ambrose, who used to sit on this very spot, surveying a scene that had not changed and would never change. Daniel used to say that Ambrose was a misguided romantic; that he saw his neighbours sharing certain articles in common and imagined he could help himself to their turf, potatoes and eggs according to his need. In romanticising both place and people, he had fallen in love with an ideal that could not be matched by the life around him. In Daniel's phrase, all experience, including the simplest things, underwent a process of multiplication in his magnifying mind. Even the fox he'd seen from the boat wasn't any old fox but a mythological character in vulpine form; and the poteen Muiris gave him on the mountain was nothing less than a draught from an Irish Hippocrene. How was he to know that the things he found or made so extraordinary in his writing were commonplace to his more knowing neighbours?

Looking around at the grey, striated cliffs, Jim tried to imagine the lone-wolf impulse that had drawn Ambrose to this wild, inhospitable place. At the time he had seen him as one of those self-haunted Englishmen who seek assuagement in the austerity of mountain and desert. Now he knew that Ambrose was not to be captured in a sub-editor's cliché. In a curious way he was as mysterious as the place he would have made his own; he was as much part of these rocks and cliffs as Paddy Canty, Muiris, Red Miller and the others. Unlike them, he was a ghost that refused to rest.